# DARE TO
# *Resist*

## A WEDDING DARE NOVELLA

# LAURA KAYE

Entangled Publishing, LLC
2614 South Timberline Road
Suite 109
Fort Collins, CO 80525
Visit our website at www.entangledpublishing.com.

Brazen is an imprint of Entangled Publishing, LLC. For more information on our titles, visit www.brazenbooks.com.

Edited by Heather Howland
Cover design by Heather Howland

Manufactured in the United States of America

First Edition May 2014

*Here's to hoping every one of you finds your happy beginning…*

# Chapter One

Kady Dresco had just kicked some major ass. She'd probably never done a better job giving a presentation. As she'd spoken, she'd literally seen the officers' enthusiasm for her proposals as they'd sat forward in their seats, asked smart, engaged questions, and then sat back, nodding and satisfied with her answers. Though she was totally squeeing and fist-pumping and Elaine-dancing on the inside, she contained her excitement as she closed PowerPoint, gathered her presentation materials, and stood at the head of the conference table.

"Thank you for the opportunity to present today," Kady said, her heart thumping against her breastbone, especially as a crash of thunder punctuated her words. Rain drummed a steady beat on the roof and windows as she glanced around the long table, making eye contact with the group of army officers responsible for hiring someone to head up the creation and installation of special computer security

programs for a new army training facility in the middle
of the Nevada desert. The room in which she stood, like
the building and the entire base, was brand-new and still
under construction, which was why the only decor were
the American and army flags standing on tall poles in one
corner.

"Very impressive, Miss Dresco," Colonel Jepsen said,
rising from his chair and extending his hand. The camouflaged
sleeve of the older man's combat uniform reminded her
for the hundredth time that her biggest competition for
this contract—not to mention biggest nemesis since she
was a kid—had the advantage of being former military.
Colton Brooks, her brother Tyler's best friend. But Kady
had innovation and sheer coding genius on her side, and
right now, she was looking forward to a little good-natured
gloating when she saw him.

"Thank you," Kady said, forcing her mind back to the
task at hand—sealing the deal. She shook the colonel's
hand and met his hard blue gaze. "I'd be happy to write up
a contract for your review tonight if we have an agreement,
sir. Do we?"

For a split second, surprise widened his eyes and lifted
his eyebrows, then he smiled and squeezed her hand a little
harder. "I like your attitude. We'll move as fast as we can on
this decision and be in touch soon. You can count on that."

Kady smiled, gathered her things, and said a round of
good-byes to the two majors, one captain, and one second
lieutenant in the room. Then, as a booming clap of thunder
shook the building, she followed the colonel out of the
conference room, through what would eventually be the
suite of offices housing the base's top brass, to a reception

area where her competition sat.

Two men who couldn't be more different in every way.

Albert Beckstein, a round little man who sweated even when it was cool and who always took potshots aimed at making her feel like she couldn't possibly know as much about computer security as someone who'd pulled off the biggest hack of 1991 and emerged on the other side of a prison sentence to build a career in computer security. That she'd been a toddler then only made her a bigger target, as far as Beckstein was concerned. Not that Kady cared what the little weasel of a man thought, especially since they both knew she'd hacked past two of his security systems, enabling her to steal a contract right out from under him just last year.

No. Albert Beckstein was good in his own by-the-book way, but he wasn't her *true* competition.

Her gaze swung to the wall of windows where Colton Brooks stood staring out at the driving rain. Before this trip, she hadn't laid eyes on him since she'd gone home for the holidays six months before. Every time she saw him, the pure masculine appeal of the man sucker punched her anew, as if while separated her mind blocked out the memory of him out of self-preservation. But, God, he was beyond gorgeous when he wasn't talking. So gorgeous she could almost forget he was the most exasperating man on the planet. The navy suit jacket emphasized the breadth of his shoulders and his still-trim waist, even three years after retiring from the military. Though you could tell the guy was *fit*, the suit did nothing to reveal just how damn ripped he was. But she'd seen *and* felt it with her own eyes and hands, and no matter how hard she tried, she couldn't make herself forget it.

As he turned, she caught the square cut of his strong

jaw and the muscle there that always ticked when he was irritated with her, as he must've been now. And then those intense brown eyes were on her, evaluating and surveying her like he could read her thoughts and command her body as he'd once done several years ago…

*Not going there, Kady. Ever again. Right.*

In addition to all that, the guy wasn't just pretty to look at. He was a decorated war hero *and* one of the best minds in their field. Just, you know, not as good as her. She smiled to herself as she drank him in, from dark-brown hair to black dress shoes. Yep, he was all that and a bag of chips. Man, how she'd love to eat him up and lick her fingers clean.

"Finally done?" Colton asked, arching a brow.

Kady smirked and ignored the question, since she'd waited through their presentations *and* ignoring Colton had the bonus of being one of the best ways to goad him, and turned to the colonel. "Thank you for the opportunity to speak with you and your staff. It was a very engaging conversation, and I look forward to working with you." She shook the man's hand again and he gave her a smile. This job was *so* hers. She basked in the rising irritation she could almost feel pouring off the other two men.

"I'll be in touch," Colonel Jepsen said. "Gentlemen." He gave the men a nod and retreated into the office suite. Thunder rumbled and lightning flashed bright enough to reflect off the wall in front of Kady.

"How'd it go, Barbie?" Beckstein said as he hoisted himself from his seat and lifted an ancient briefcase into his beefy palm.

Kady *tsk*ed. "Al," she said using the nickname she knew he hated. "Don't you know anything? Barbie was blond and would've been at least five nine. At five three and with black hair, I'm much more of a…Catwoman." She walked up to him and could nearly look him in the eyes he was so short. "You have something…" She grimaced and pointed to a crumb stuck to his tie. He batted it away with a deep frown. "Yes, so feel free to call me Selina, if you can't remember Kady. I'd be happy to be named after a character who was a great *thief*," she said with a pause she knew he'd understand since he'd accused her of that very thing last year, "and a great crime-fighter."

Colton's stifled snicker behind her made the treat of dressing down Beckstein all the sweeter, especially as the little man's face turned beet red. Not everyone in her field was the outright arrogant, sexist asshole Beckstein was, but she'd gotten used to dealing with men who didn't take her seriously in professional situations. Turned out being a young, petite woman mattered more to some people than the fact that she could write complex code half asleep and with one arm tied behind her back. That was part of the reason she needed to win this contract. It was exactly the feather in the cap of her portfolio that would garner her the respect—and the promotion—she deserved in her firm.

"Now," she said, turning to the man she'd crushed on since about the time she got her first bra. *Crushed.* As in, in the past. Not anymore. Nope. "Do you want to call the transport driver or should I?" Because the facility was new, a few miles from a one-stoplight town, and required special clearances to enter, a driver had been assigned to shuttle them from the airport nearly ninety minutes away to the base and back again after all their presentations were complete. The three of them represented the finalist companies in what she understood had been a quite competitive request for proposals.

"No need," he said, making a big show of checking the chunky black military watch he wore. How a watch could be so damn sexy, Kady didn't know. But the simple movement — from the flick of his wrist that hiked up his suit coat to the way the muscle on his forearm popped — was pure masculine poetry in motion. Bastard. "He's been here for nearly half an hour. We've all been *waiting*." Colton's eyebrow arched again as he retrieved his laptop case from a chair.

Kady suppressed an eye roll. "Oh, well. Why didn't you say so? Come on already," she said, heading into the hallway and feeling Colton's gaze bore into her back. "And don't blame me that my presentation went longer. I can't help it if they were totally engaged by my plans."

"Sure they weren't asking questions because you'd talked over their heads and left them confused?" Beckstein asked from behind her.

Kady scoffed and tossed a glance over her shoulder. "You know as well as I do that I'm the best there is at boiling complicated concepts into completely accessible explanations, Al. So keep dreaming if it makes you feel better."

No response. Exactly. She smiled at Beckstein's silence.

Walking right beside her, Colton was like a big, gorgeous, brooding mountain. She glanced his way, and sure enough, he was staring down at her in that intense and penetrating way he had. The heat of a flush crawled up her neck. "What?" she asked, hating that he didn't even have to say anything to get under her skin.

He pressed his lips together and shook his head, which of

course drew her gaze to his mouth and made her remember how he —

*Nope. Don't go there.* She blew out a deep breath.

They continued down the hall, the click of her heels on the tile floor and the intermittent thunder the only sounds. Finally, they entered a large rectangular lobby decorated with flags and portraits of the president and the base's commanding officer.

A young soldier stood by the glass front doors talking on his cell phone. He turned when he heard them and gave a nod. "Yes. I understand. What about going east across—" He paused. "Roger that. I'll take them there." He lowered the phone and approached, a troubled expression on his young face. "Sirs, ma'am, I'm afraid we have a hiccup in the plans."

"What is it, Soldier?" Colton asked.

The guy gestured toward the doors. "Looks like monsoon season came a little early this year, sir," he said. "The storm's washed out the roads, which doesn't matter much since the airport's grounded all flights for the rest of the day due to the wind and lightning."

Kady frowned and mentally ran damage control on tomorrow's schedule.

"That's not a hiccup. That's a disaster," Beckstein said, mopping his brow. "I have work to do. A company to run. What exactly are we supposed to do now?" He turned on her. "This is all your fault."

She inhaled to respond when Colton held a hand up to Beckstein. "That's not helping anyone, *Al*," he said.

Kady bit the inside of her cheek to keep from laughing at the little man's scowl. She shouldn't like the way Colton always stood up for her, especially when his sense of duty to her older brother played a role in the behavior, but she supposed it was mildly endearing. Sometimes.

"So what's plan B?" Colton asked the soldier.

"I've been authorized to take you to the motel in town whenever you're ready." He slipped his phone into his pocket.

"Lead the way," Colton said, tucking his bag under the flap of his suit coat.

Kady sighed as she followed the soldier out the door and into wind blowing so hard the rain pelted sideways. Hugging her bags to her chest to protect her laptop, she ran for the white government van knowing no matter how fast she moved she was going to be soaked. This was one of those times when it was a good thing she wasn't high maintenance.

"Think it'll rain today?" Colton called over the deluge.

Kady couldn't hold back a smile. "It's the freaking desert, Brooks. Never rains here." She clambered into the van's middle seat, her feet floating in her heels and her cute white blouse plastered to her skin. Which reminded her that she didn't have any other clothes with her.

Maybe there was a store in town where she could pick up a few basics? If not, she'd be putting the blow-dryer to good use so she at least had something to sleep in. No matter. It was just one night. She could make do. As long as she had her laptop and her personal hot spot, she could be happy just about anywhere.

When Beckstein took the front passenger seat, Colton tugged the sliding door to the back shut and shifted into the seat in front of her. He gazed over his shoulder, his mouth half open with some smart-ass comment no doubt, when he did a double take and turned toward her, a scowl darkening his expression. The next thing she knew he was shrugging out of his suit jacket and handing it over the seat to her. "Put this on," he said in a low voice. "*Now*."

"Excuse me?" she said. His bossiness was totally *not* one of his more endearing qualities.

He arched a brow and gave her a pointed look.

Kady gazed down at herself. *Oh. Oh, shit.* The rain had turned the crisp cotton of her favorite white button-down with the square neckline and the ruffle collar absolutely sheer. So sheer the pattern in the lace of her bra showed through. Meeting his gaze again, she rolled her eyes but accepted the jacket. "Thanks," she said, muscling back any embarrassment. After all, it wasn't like this was the first time he'd seen her breasts.

Before she had the suit coat halfway on, she already knew agreeing to wear it was a huge mistake. Because it smelled frickin' *fantastic*. Like clean soap and spicy aftershave and something entirely Colton—in other words, something entirely intoxicating. Her mouth watered and her heart raced, and that irritated her because *damnit* she hated that he had this kind of power over her body. And it wasn't even *him* touching her. Not that he would. Or that she would let him.

She was pretty sure he'd met and exceeded her tolerance for humiliation this decade, thank you very much. Not that she cared anymore. Their one night together was ancient history as far as she was concerned. And she'd be surprised if he ever thought of it at all.

"It's wet," she said as the rain-chilled wool settled on her shoulders.

"Not as wet as you," he murmured.

She gaped up at him and...yup. His blazing eyes and ticking jaw told her he was fully aware of the double entendre of his words—and that those words had the power to heat her cheeks—and other places. Kady bit down on the snarky response that flew to the tip of her tongue: *Wouldn't you like to know?* Colton had always given good banter, but why the hell was he pulling out the innuendo when he'd been the one to back off and decide the two of them together was a bad idea? She tugged the jacket closed. It was so big, it easily crossed over her chest in overlapping layers. "Happy?"

"Ecstatic," he deadpanned, lips pressed tight and eyes narrowed. As the van got under way, he glanced forward, allowing her to drink in his profile. The rain had turned his hair nearly black and she had to fist her hands against the urge to catch the droplets of water running down his jaw with her fingers. Or her tongue.

They hit an alignment-destroying rut in the road and Kady threw out her arms to steady herself on a surprised cry. One hand grasped the back of the seat in front of her, brushing Colton's forearm in the process.

His gaze cut back to her and his eyes narrowed at the gap in the front of the suit jacket her position had created. "Better hold on tight, cupcake."

"Oh, don't worry, *Colt*, I will," she said, returning his annoying term of endearment with the nickname she knew he found equally grating. His gaze was almost a physical caress on her face and breasts, but Kady refused to meet it because she didn't want him to see that his words had affected her again. But in truth, the stupid little term of endearment curled anger into her belly because it took her right back to the night three years before when the competitiveness and tension between them had flashed red hot and led to the single most intense sexual experience of her life. And they hadn't even had sex. Not because she hadn't wanted to, but because Colton had developed second thoughts and declared the whole thing a mistake.

The wheels caught in another pothole that tossed Kady in her seat.

Their hookup had happened at the party welcoming Colton home from the military. Before that night, she'd only seen him now and then when he'd come home on leave and hung out with her brother. But that night, from the moment she'd seen Colton out on the back deck leaning against the railing, beer in hand and absolutely glorious smile on his suntanned face, he'd totally stolen her breath. During his two tours in the army, he'd gone from a gorgeous boy to an incredibly hot man who had the filled-out, muscular body, survival skills, and wartime experiences to justify the arrogance that had always been part of his personality. Her friend Regan, who had a knack for summing people up in just three words, didn't refer to Colton as a loyal, driven badass for nothing.

Kady could certainly agree with the "ass" part anyway.

"*Well, damn. Is that really you, cupcake?*" Those were the first words he'd said to her that night. The nickname had been cute for about five minutes when she'd been, like, thirteen, and afterward he'd continued to call her that simply because he knew it annoyed her.

And though she'd teased right back that eight years in the military apparently hadn't changed him at all, it hadn't taken her long to realize that wasn't actually the case. Because all night, Colton had *looked* at her differently. Like, for the first time in their lives, he actually saw *her*, and not just Tyler's little sister. Her. Kady. The twenty-three-year-old woman.

After hours of circling each other and subtle glances that had turned more brazen the later it had gotten, he'd walked into the pool house after she'd changed into her bikini and stared at her like a starving man at a feast. "*Problem?*" she'd asked. And his answer to the question had been to close them in one of the dressing rooms, kiss her senseless, and make her scream his name not once but twice, first with his thick fingers and then with his mouth. God, between his dirty talk and rough handling he'd had her so out of her mind she'd freaking begged for him to fuck her. In that moment, nothing else had mattered but him burying himself as deep inside her as he could go.

Then her brother—who had the gift of perhaps the worst timing in the history of man—had come looking for Colton, and the sound of Tyler's voice had totally thrown Colton out of the moment and sent him flailing back from her like she was a snake that might strike him down.

What was worse was that, in college, Regan and Kady's sorority sister Christine had predicted that outcome—both how incendiary Kady and Colton would be if they ever gave in to the chemistry brewing between them *and* the fact that he'd pull a duck and cover. Which was exactly what he'd done. But had Kady listened? Nope. She'd led with her body instead of her brain and gotten her heart stomped on for her trouble.

*Ugh, whatever.*

Thunder crashed above them, pulling Kady out of the memory. She wished she could make out some detail of the passing scenery through the rain-blurred windows because she really didn't need to dwell on how he'd commanded her body that night, nor on the humiliating words he'd said afterward. Not with the man himself sitting two feet in front of her.

Besides, young girl crush aside, it wasn't like she had *feelings* for him or anything. Despite the fact that he was the only man who'd ever been able to get her off. She could take care of herself just fine, but other men? Kady didn't know if Colton had ruined her or held the only key to her lock, but either way, it didn't matter. She could *never* get there no matter how hard she—or her lovers—tried. At this rate, it might be a wise financial investment to buy stock in Duracell.

Kady's cheeks caught on absolute fire at the thought. *Sitting. In. Front. Of. You. Dresco.* Right. No more thinking about orgasms or lack thereof in the presence of the infuriating sex god. Got it.

Needing a distraction, Kady pulled out her iPhone and thumbed open her email. She needed to let Christine know she wouldn't be home today so she wouldn't worry, but the little loading icon spun and spun but never actually produced any new emails. She tried her social media accounts and found more of the same. With a sigh, she dropped the phone back into her purse.

As the rain drummed on the van's metal roof, Kady imagined the gorgeous weather she'd no doubt be enjoying back home in southern San Fran. Her firm, Resnick Security Services, was headquartered in California's Silicon Valley. She loved living near the Pacific Ocean, visiting the wineries, and going out with Christine and their girlfriends to all the amazing restaurants in the city, but she still missed the mountains of Boulder where she'd grown up and her family still lived.

Finally, another series of harsh bounces had them turning into the lot of the Desert Paradise Motel. Through the windows, she could just make out the long one-story, cinder-block building with doors facing the parking lot. At one end sat a small office, and beyond that a bright-orange roof covered what appeared to be a diner. Seemed to her the ratio between *desert* and *paradise* at the place was just a bit off.

The soldier brought the van to a stop and turned around in the driver's seat. "The travel office booked you reservations here, so you'll need to give them a credit card for incidentals, but the rooms are covered with late checkout. Assuming the roads reopen, we have you booked on the same evening flights tomorrow. Those are the first available. So, if Mother Nature cooperates, I'll be here at fifteen hundred to take you to the airport."

Colton nodded. "Roger that."

"This place is the best you can do?" Beckstein asked, a sneer on his little round face.

The soldier didn't take the bait and instead smiled. Kady wanted to give him a high five. "Yes, sir. Before the base, Panther Canyon was little more than a crossroads. This is the only motel in town until the new Best Western is finished."

Beckstein released a long-suffering sigh. "Whole day lost," he grumbled as he scrambled out of the van and into the rain.

Kady scooted to the edge of her seat and slipped her purse and laptop case under her arm where Colton's coat would help keep them dry. "Sorry about him," she called. "It's not your fault it's raining."

The soldier grinned. "Thank you, ma'am." He pointed out the front window. "The diner over there has decent burgers and great milk shakes if y'all get hungry later."

"Sounds good," Colton said, hauling open the sliding door. Wind and rain blew in so hard it made Kady catch her breath. Colton jumped out, his back hunched to offer some protection to his own computer, and offered Kady a hand. See? Sometimes, he could actually be a gentleman.

"Thank you," she called to the driver as she accepted Colton's hand. "And thank you, too," she said to Colton.

"Did…did I hear Kady Dresco just thank *me*?" he asked, humor playing around his eyes and mouth.

Kady stepped down, the force of the rain making it hard to give him a good smirk. "Yes, but now I'm regretting it," she said just as her foot sank into a deep, cold puddle, throwing her off-balance.

She wobbled on her heels and Colton caught her with a hand on her ribs. "Okay?" he asked, dark eyes gazing down at her so intensely that for a moment she barely felt the rain on her face and shoulders.

"Yeah. Fine." She pulled her hand free. She might find him irritating 90 percent of the time, but it was better to keep contact to a minimum, especially when he managed a bit of sweetness or charm. Because *sweet* and *Colton* equaled a lethal cocktail she'd never been able to resist.

Colton closed the door and then they dashed the short way across the lot to the entrance to the office. Kady could've sworn he kept a hand on the small of her back, as if he stood at the ready in case the combination of her three-inch heels and the two-inch-deep puddles made her unsteady again.

Beckstein pushed out of the door as they reached it, and of course he didn't let them in first. What a ginormous asswipe.

Finally, they made it in out of the rain and stood dripping on the old linoleum floor of the tiny office.

"You can check in first," Colton said, running a hand through his wet hair.

Kady's phone rang. "Oh. Go ahead," she said as she dug for the cell. Her assistant launched into a rundown of client calls before Kady stopped her. "Can you put all of this in an email to me? I'm stranded here overnight due to a storm, but if you send me everything I'll return any calls I can today and all the rest tomorrow. Oh, and can you email Carson and copy me so we can reschedule the site visit I was supposed to do tomorrow?" A few more housekeeping matters kept her on the phone for another minute or two before she hung up and approached the registration desk just as Colton finished.

The man on the other side of the ancient, stained counter was quite possibly as old as the desert itself. He pushed his glasses up, then stared down his nose at her. "Welcome to paradise," he said with a straight face.

Kady burst out laughing before she could stop herself. She slapped a hand over her mouth. "Sorry," she said.

He blinked lazily, as if she hadn't just made an ass of herself. "Can I help you?"

"Right. Yes. I'm Kady Dresco. I'm with the guys who just checked in." She glanced over her shoulder toward Colton, who stood by the door shaking his head at her. "What?" she mouthed.

"Here you go, missy." In almost slow motion, and without

really taking his gaze off the small television that sat to the side, the receptionist lifted a key off a row of hooks and pushed it across the counter to her. Before long, she was all checked in and held an actual metal key on a ring in her hand. The large plastic tag read "2."

"Are there any stores that might sell clothing nearby?" she asked.

The man squinted for a moment, then shook his head. "Not unless you want something from the tack shop, which is about five miles from here. Otherwise, nearest shopping is in Battle Mountain. Won't get there in this weather, though."

About what Kady expected. Oh, well. Looked like she had an appointment with a hair dryer, after all. "Okay, thanks."

Colton held up his key chain as she crossed the room toward him. "At least you won't be able to forget your room number," he said with a smirk.

"Shut up," she said. You forget your room number and try to enter someone else's room on *one* family vacation—of course, one where your brother's hot best friend tags along—and you never live it down.

"Good comeback." He winked as he pushed the door open for her.

Kady rolled her eyes as she sidestepped past him and out into the humid June afternoon. A narrow sidewalk skirted close to the building from the office around to the long row of guest rooms. Rain fell in a sheet over the edge of the obviously overworked gutter. It was almost like walking behind a waterfall. "This is me," Kady said at the second room.

"I'm in ten," he said, gesturing past her. "Do you mind?"

"What? Oh," she said. The sidewalk wasn't wide enough for him to get around her without getting caught in the downpour. "Not afraid of a little rain, are ya?" He just looked at her. She grinned as she slipped the key into the lock and pushed open her door.

Kady froze.

It was raining. Inside her room. From about a half dozen places on the ceiling, water dripped at speeds ranging from Chinese water torture to what could only be described as a steady stream. The latter was right over the only bed in the room.

From behind her, she heard a low, male chuckle. "Not afraid of a little rain, are ya?"

# Chapter Two

Colton Brooks couldn't hold back laughing as Kady's expression shifted from surprised to downright horrified. Really, he appreciated just about any reason to throw her off-kilter. Teasing and one-upmanship had always been their style, especially as her innate coding and hacking abilities emerged during her teenage years while he was six years older and busting his ass to master what came to her naturally. And since her older brother, Tyler, had been one of his best friend since…forever, Colton and Kady had been thrown together enough over the years to fuel the flames of their rivalry.

Fortunately, nowadays, that rivalry served the strategically important purpose of distracting Colton from what he'd otherwise be thinking about, especially now that Kady was all grown up—which was stripping her down and claiming her in every way a man could claim a woman.

Despite the fact that the very sexy real thing was standing

an arm's length away, a three-year-old image flashed into his mind's eye. Kady's face up close in the dimness of the pool house. Mouth open and eyes pleading as he boxed her up against the wall, restrained her hands above her head, and got her off with his fingers while his cock strained against her belly.

The memory was a sucker punch to the gut and shot blood southward.

*Cut it out, Brooks.*

Hot as that night had been and as often as it ran through the solitude of his thoughts, it had been a mistake then. And it remained one now. For a whole fucking host of reasons.

So, since he couldn't give in to what he really wanted from Kady Dresco, he picked on her and snarked at her and generally gave her grief. And she gave it right back. None of it was ever mean-spirited and he suspected she enjoyed it every bit as much as he did. Sometimes he thought they were engaged in one long round of mental foreplay. Except they could never—*would* never—seal the deal.

Because Kady deserved a helluva lot better than him.

Colton stepped into the room right behind Kady and surveyed the water damage, which was much safer than admiring the way she looked in his jacket. No way he should like that as much as he did—or that he should take even an iota of satisfaction from the idea that his scent was now all over her. He cleared his throat. "You don't even have to get out of bed to take a shower. Really, it's such a time saver."

The fiery green of her gaze cut to his face. "You are so funny, I can hardly breathe for the laughter," she said with a completely straight face.

"Ooh, touchy," he said, fighting back the smile that

threatened.

She held out her key. "You like it so much, I'm happy to trade."

He shook his head and let the smile loose. "Not a chance, Dresco."

Kady rolled her eyes. "Uh-huh. Out of my way, then," she said, pushing against his stomach and stepping past him.

He fisted his hands to restrain himself from acting on the urge to trap her against him, his fingers pressing into her soft skin. And right there was part of the problem where they were concerned—his sexual interests veered to the rough side. Definitely not the kind of thing you did to a nice girl six years your junior who you'd known when she wore pigtails and who was one of your best friends' little sister. And even if Colton could get past all that, he couldn't see Kady putting up with being manhandled and controlled in bed for even one minute.

"Sonofabitch," he muttered beneath his breath as he forced his body under control and followed Kady back around the sidewalk to the office. She glanced over her shoulder, a question clear in those beautiful eyes. He hiked his computer case higher on his shoulder and pretended not to notice.

Inside, Kady marched up to the desk and laid her key on the counter. "Excuse me?"

"Welcome to paradise," the old man said. Kady didn't laugh this time, though she did make an *Oh my God, would you get a load of this guy?* face over her shoulder at him. "Oh, you again, missy?" Colton smiled to himself as he imagined her reaction if he called her missy.

"Yes, sir. It's raining in my room. I need another."

The man cupped his hand to his ear. "Eh?"

"It's raining in my current room," she said slower and louder. "Can I please get a different room?"

For a long moment, the old dude just stared at her. No discernible reaction. "Oh, that's right," he finally said with a slow nod. "Two has a leak."

Colton coughed to hide his laugh and covered his mouth with his fist.

"Um, with all due respect, sir. It's *raining* in room two. As in, actual rain. In the room. On the furniture. On the carpet. On the bed." She offered a hand motion that was apparently meant to illustrate the point.

The man stared at her hand like it might reveal the meaning of life and then shrugged when it didn't. "I just work the desk, but I'll let 'em know."

Kady looked back at Colton with a totally bewildered expression on her face. He gave her a wink.

"Uh, okay," she said as she tucked her long, wavy black hair behind her ears. It was longer than when he'd last seen her at Christmas, which made it even sexier. His hand twitched at the memory of how soft and thick her hair was, not to mention the thought of how damn good it would feel fisted in his hand while he—

"So, have any rooms without a leak?" she asked.

"O' course," the man said, glancing at the television. "Except we don't have any vacancies."

She settled her purse and laptop bag on the counter. "You mean—"

"Booked," the guy said, pointing at a long row of empty hooks on the wall above him. Colton hadn't realized the significance of that emptiness when he'd checked in because it hadn't mattered then. He glanced out the door and saw the blurred shapes and colors of cars parked here and there along the front of the building. And then he recalled the private who drove them here saying this motel represented the only accommodations in town. His stomach began the long, slow crawl into his boots.

"There must be something you can do," she said, the first real hint of being upset slipping into her voice.

"Wish there was," he said.

Kady's fists curled around the straps to her bags and she looked down as if collecting herself. "Okay," she whispered, her shoulders rising and falling as if she'd taken a deep breath. "Thanks, anyway," she said as she glanced up again. Grabbing her things, she slowly walked across the office. "Well…"

An idea came to mind, and as revolting as it was, it was miles better than the alternative. "Uh, sir?" he asked, approaching the counter. "Can you tell me what room my friend is in? Albert Beckstein?"

"Seven," the man said, not looking away from the television.

Good to know security was rock-solid here. But at least they didn't have to go knocking. "Come on," he said to Kady as he hit the door.

"Wait. You're gonna—"

"Bunk with Beckstein. Only reasonable solution," he said, glad that the narrow sidewalk forced them to walk single file. That way he couldn't see whatever expression she might be wearing right now. Because anything in the neighborhood of disappointment or disagreement might do very bad things to his self-control. And anything that resembled happiness would just make him pissed off. Not a fair reaction, since he'd been the one to shut them down—hard. But there it was all the same.

Toward the far end of the building, she came to a stop in front of the door marked number seven and turned to him.

Ah, motherfucker. Her expression was part confused, part concerned, and the frown shaping those pretty red lips looked a helluva lot like disappointment to him.

Not letting his brain churn on what her reaction might mean, Colton knocked on the door. Being locked in a room with Albert freaking Beckstein would be a lot less painful than sharing the same space with the star of his darkest fantasies while not being able to touch her. That was for damn sure.

No answer. Colton knocked again.

Kady stepped closer. "Colton, we can just—"

Fist, meet door. This time the knock was more of a bang.

The door swung open. "What?" Beckstein said.

"I, uh…" Colton's words trailed off as he noticed three things in quick succession. Beckstein's pants were not fully secured. A bottle of what Colton guessed was lotion or something similar lay on the floor behind the guy. And a box of tissues and his open laptop lay near where pillows were propped against the headboard on the rumpled bed.

Holy mother of fucking hell.

Colton's stomach churned. It was one thing to jack off. It was another thing to jack off and not secure your shit before you opened a goddamned door. That was like, Puberty 101. Or Being a Guy 101. Or Basic Fucking Common Sense 101.

"I'm busy. What do you want?" Beckstein said, zipping himself.

Kady gripped Colton's arm. "Nothing. We, uh, just wanted to tell you the diner over there is supposed to have good food," she said as a sense of doom closed in over Colton.

Colton shook his head, rejecting what she was trying to do—namely, rescue him—even as he appreciated the gesture. But damnit, he'd faced down jumping out of airplanes and deadly insurgents and IEDs and living in a hot, sandy hell for months on end. He could damn well handle one disgusting, grating, but otherwise harmless computer nerd for a night.

*Right. So get your ass in there before Kady convinces him—and more importantly you—that you didn't come here for anything more than a restaurant recommendation.*

Beckstein huffed. "Diner. Good. Yeah, yeah, got it." His beady-eyed gaze bounced between the pair of them for another moment, and then he stepped back and closed the door in their faces.

And Colton was immediately saved from torture and damned to hell.

* * *

"I think I just threw up in my mouth," Kady said, still kinda stunned. She tugged the lapels of Colton's coat tighter around her, as if it could shield her from what'd just happened. Who the hell answered the door when they were in the middle of masturbating? And, if you had to answer the door, who didn't hide every last scrap of evidence of said masturbation first??? Albert freaking Beckstein. That's who. "Am I crazy, or did we just…was he just—"

"Yeah." Colton scrubbed a hand over his face. "Never speak of this again."

Kady chuckled and leaned her head against the thick bulge of Colton's arm, making her realize she still had a death grip on his biceps from when she'd been trying to warn him away. Since touching him when she now had to share a room with him probably wasn't the best idea, she let him go and stepped back. A flock of butterflies whipped through her belly. "Well, you dodged a bullet, Brooks," she said, acting like she wasn't nervous and excited and really freaking nervous. "Looks like you're stuck with me." She peered up at him from beneath her lashes…and tried not to get her feelings hurt that he didn't look particularly happy about that fact. But, damn, if he thought rooming with her was worse than rooming with Beckstein, that didn't say much about his opinion of her, did it?

A memory sucked her three years back in time.

*After Tyler left the pool house, Colton retrieved his shirt from the floor of the dressing room and refused to meet her gaze. "I didn't mean for this to happen. You were just…there, and it's been a long time."*

*Humiliation heated Kady's face. God. If Tyler hadn't walked in, she would've had sex with Colton—and* this *was what he thought of her? "What? Like, I was just any warm body?" she said, embarrassment shivering over her nakedness as his words battered against the affection she'd always felt for him, even when he made her crazy. "Like this wasn't about me and you? Wow. And I thought you'd actually seen me tonight."*

*Anger darkened his expression. "Of course I see you. I've always seen you."*

*"No, you haven't," she said, crossing her arms over her breasts. It would take too long to fix the ties on her bikini top,*

*and she didn't feel like swimming anymore now anyway. Or staying at this party for a second longer. "You've always seen Tyler's sister."*

*He threw out his hands. "Well, you are Tyler's little sister. What the hell do you want from me?"*

*"Not a thing." Kady scooped up her top and paused, her hand on the dressing room door. "But think about what you just said, Brooks. You have no idea who I am."*

*"Yeah? Well, you don't know me, either."*

*"Clearly," she said, and then she slipped out the door.*

"You okay?" Colton asked, expression serious.

Kady blinked out of the memory and shook off the phantom pain of the exchange. That was old news and she'd gotten over it, and they'd seen each other enough times since that night that awkwardness no longer lingered. "Yep," she said, giving him a smile. "Ready to go see what lurks behind door number three?"

Colton tapped the plastic key chain against his hand. "Guess we better before the moaning starts."

Chuckling, Kady turned and dashed toward Colton's room—*their* room, now. "God forbid," she called over her shoulder. "Bad enough I'll have the image in my head. I don't need the soundtrack. Hurry up."

Colton walked toward her slowly, and though she was cold and wet and freaking out just a little, she couldn't deny the way his almost calculated approach made her belly flip-flop. Tall, dark, beautiful, brooding... But not for her. Didn't hurt to look though, did it? Her gaze dragged over the lean muscles of his body. Nope, didn't hurt at all.

He jingled the key, then slipped it in the lock. "Here goes nothing." The door swung open and he flicked at the light switch just inside.

"Oh," Kady said. "Looks like third time's a charm." In the positive column was the fact that it was a rain-and-masturbator-free room. In the negative column was the fact that there was just one bed. As in, one. For both of them. She stepped inside, dropped her bags onto the little round table in front of the window, and slipped out of Colton's coat.

The door clicked shut behind her and Colton settled his bag on the floor beside a chair. He lingered by the door for a long moment, hands on his hips as his gaze surveyed the typical motel accommodations. Did this room feel small or did Colton just seem to take up a lot of it? He took off his shoes, then turned on a few lamps, peeked into the bathroom, and generally checked things out.

Kady stepped out of her waterlogged heels, but then didn't know what to do with herself. The rain drummed on the roof loud enough to compete with the *whirr* of the air-conditioning unit, which chilled her wet blouse and made her shiver. What she really wanted was a hot shower, but given the odd tension hanging in the air like a fog, she thought it might be a little early to start getting naked. "Well," she said, shoving away the thought of Colton totally bared to her eyes. "I think I'll check some email and return some calls."

Colton ran his hand through his hair. "Yeah. Me, too. No doubt my in-box has exploded in the last eight hours."

Taking a seat at the table, Kady smiled as she unpacked her laptop. "Guess that's what happens when you're the boss man, huh?" Two years ago, he'd opened his own computer security services firm in Boulder and immediately won contracts working with the military and defense contractors who prized his experience with the army's Cyber Command both in the States and while deployed on field teams overseas. Truth be told, Kady envied the autonomy he had working for himself.

"Like you wouldn't believe. But I haven't found anyone I want to take on as a partner, yet." With a sigh, he grabbed his laptop bag and settled into the chair across from her. A flash of lightning threw shadows over the table for a moment. "I brought a surge protector if you want to plug into that," he said.

"That's so awesome I'm not even going to crack a Boy Scout joke. This storm is crazy."

Colton gave her a droll smile. "Your restraint is unparalleled."

*Ha! You have no idea, Colton. I'm trapped in a tiny room with the only man I know who's capable of giving me an orgasm and I haven't jumped him.* Kady smiled to herself as she bent under the table to plug in her power cord, then she set up her laptop and hot spot and logged in to her firm's network. She ran through a few easy emails and peeked over the top of her screen at her roommate. Brow furrowed in concentration, his brown eyes moved as if he were reading. She watched him for a moment, struck by the fact that it was...kinda nice to be sitting here working with him like this.

Though they did the same kind of work and saw each other at conferences and occasionally when competing for contracts, like today, it had been years since they'd actually worked on anything together. One of the first times had been when he'd come home to her house with Tyler for Thanksgiving his sophomore year in college. His parents' marriage had been a total train wreck and Colton and his sister, Sophie, had never seemed like their first priority, so occasionally the Brooks siblings would end up at the Dresco house for a holiday meal. Kady's mom loved hosting them both, and having Sophie around, even as shy as she was, gave Kady someone to hang with besides the annoying boys.

But that particular Thanksgiving, Colton had been entirely stressed out over a final project on network protection. Curious what college-level computer assignments might look like, Kady had sneaked into Tyler's room when Colton had taken a break and looked over his materials. He hadn't been happy when he'd caught her going through his notes until she made a few suggestions that helped him solve his research problem. They'd worked on it together the rest of that night.

His gaze cut to hers. "Why are you watching me?"

Busted. Kady ducked her chin to hide the heat filling her face. "Pfft. Get over yourself. I'm not watching you." Her fingers flew over the keyboard as she answered another email.

"Uh-huh. I think you missed me, Dresco," he said, that old arrogance filling his tone.

She tossed an eye roll his way. "That would be like missing my dentist. Totally never happens." Another chill set her to shivering. She wished Colton's coat was dry enough to be warm, but that was going to take a while. So she went to the bathroom and grabbed one of the towels to wrap around her shoulders. Examining herself in the bathroom mirror, she looked kinda ridiculous and her hair was a wavy disaster, but at least she was warmer.

Colton's gaze tracked her as soon as she returned to the main room. "You that cold?" he asked with a frown.

"It's fine."

"She says as her teeth chatter." He pushed the top button of his dress shirt through the hole and worked downward.

She couldn't tear her gaze away. "What are you—"

"I'm gonna turn on the heat long enough to dry my button-down. Then it's all yours."

"Really, I'm fine," she managed as he shrugged off the white cotton and revealed a V-neck T-shirt that did absolutely nothing to hide the contours of his muscles. Helpless to stop herself, her gaze traced over the definition of his chest, his stomach, his shoulders, his biceps. The man was cut to such perfection that it made Kady want to trace every dip and curve with her fingertips. Just to see if he was as hard as he looked. Heat lanced through her blood.

"You don't get to be a thirty-two-year-old man without learning that when a woman says she's fine, she's really not." He arched a brow that challenged her to disagree.

She smirked but kept her mouth shut because, on the one hand, he was right. And on the other, his rightness made her want to ask where that kind of wisdom had been three years ago when he'd been a total ass.

In a quick series of movements, Colton adjusted the thermostat, moved the table out from in front of the window, and draped his shirt over the back of his chair to dry. Sitting again, he scooted his chair closer to the stream of warm air rising up from the vent.

"Well, thanks," Kady said, settling back into her chair. First the coat, then offering her his room, now the shirt. Since Tyler was often around when she and Colton saw each other, she wasn't used to him stepping up to take care of her like this. Not that she was the kind of woman who needed taking care of all the time, but who didn't admire and appreciate a well-placed chivalrous gesture? Kindness was sexy.

Peering over his laptop at her, he winked. "That's twice in one day."

Leave it to Colton not to quit while he was ahead. "Don't count on a third."

His eyebrows raised in an expression of challenge. "I bet I can make you say thank you at least one more time today."

The words "I bet" froze Kady's fingers where they sat on her keyboard. She'd always had a hard time ignoring those words, especially when they came out of his mouth, as they often had over the years. And he knew it. She met his gaze and arched her brow. "The stakes?"

He tilted his head, his eyes narrowing. "Breakfast at the diner. You thank me, you buy. You don't, I buy."

Kady shrugged. This was gonna be easy as pancakes. "Why not? A new contract and free breakfast. I think I like the desert."

"Contract isn't yours yet," he said, giving her a hard stare. "And neither is breakfast."

She tugged the towel tighter around her shoulders. "Just a matter of time," she said.

He shook his head as if in exasperation, but the corners of his eyes crinkled. "Bet starts now. I think I'll eat a light dinner tonight so I'm extra hungry for breakfast."

Kady bit back a grin. "You're ridiculous. You know that, right?"

"Maybe. But you like me."

Kady inhaled to respond, but she was saved by the bell. Or rather, by the vibration of her cell phone against the veneer of the table. Her stomach dropped at the name on the caller ID. Bob Chase, her immediate supervisor at

Resnick. "Hello, this is Kady Dresco."

"I thought you were going to be back in time for the site visit with Carson tomorrow," Bob said without as much as a hello. The fact that she'd gone over his head to propose going after the project at this Panther Canyon facility had significantly moved her name up on his shit list. When she'd gotten the tip about the request for proposals here, Kady had known she couldn't go through Bob with it. He'd either block her effort or take credit for the find—or both. So she'd gone to Mr. Resnick directly with full awareness doing so would earn Bob's ire. But she'd decided it was worth the risk, and she'd been right. Resnick had been impressed enough by her identifying the job and her proposal for it that he'd given her the green light to bid as the project manager—which meant landing the contract was in essence a promotion. To not have to work for Bob Chase would be a dream come true... "If you can't...commitments on smaller projects, how do you think...to manage bigger ones like this boondoggle you're on...?"

Despite the weak cell service, Kady got the gist of Bob's tirade. And she wasn't really surprised. But boondoggle? Seriously? Was it 1953? Kady sucked down the snark and made nice. "I understand, Bob. And I apologize. There's a terrible storm here and the airport canceled—"

"None of which would've been a problem...stayed at the office," he barked.

Anger settled into Kady's chest and a multitude of responses rushed to the tip of her tongue. Like, reminding him how lucrative this contract could be, because the initial systems they wanted were just the start of a potentially long-term relationship with this facility and others like it. Like, that Resnick had given Kady his permission and blessing to be here. Or even, just maybe, that he was a giant hemorrhoid. "I understand," she said instead, forcing some sugar into her tone. "But fortunately, Carson was fine rescheduling for Friday afternoon, which actually worked better with his schedule."

Apparently deciding to ignore the most important point of their conversation—the client was actually happier with the new meeting time—Bob plowed on. "Why can't you rent a car so that you can…this meeting?"

A *click* sounded from across the table, and Kady looked up to find that Colton had closed his laptop and sat staring at her. No, scowling. And clearly listening in.

Ugh. She'd been so intent on handling Bob that she'd momentarily forgotten she wasn't having this conversation in private. She got up from the chair, crossed the room, and closed herself in the bathroom. The last impression she ever wanted Colton Brooks to have of her was that she couldn't hold her own in this field—in any and every manner.

*What part of "terrible storm" don't you understand?* she thought, as she fought to hang on to her composure. "I wish I could," she said in a tone you might use with a pouty toddler. "But there's literally nothing here. The nearest car rental is at the airport, which I can't get to."

"Something you have to learn when you're a program manager is how to manage competing time commitments. If you can't, I'll reassign Carson's project," he said. *Click.*

"Asshole!" she whispered as she braced her hands on the counter. She forced a deep breath. "He doesn't matter. None of that matters. Because you'll get the contract and then you'll be out from under him." She nodded, the pep talk releasing some of the tension in her shoulders.

Facing the door, Kady straightened her spine and relaxed her expression. She didn't want Colton to think the call had ruffled her feathers in the least. Flicking the light switch off, she opened the door and smacked face-first into six foot two inches of hard masculine flesh.

# Chapter Three

Hands braced on either side of the doorjamb, Colton stared down at Kady. God, she was a little thing. But lush, with sexy, feminine curves—the feeling of which was now emblazoned all down the front of his body from where she'd just walked into him.

"What was that about?" he asked, the heat of anger stirring in his gut. Someone had been hassling her.

"Oh," she said with a shrug that was supposed to come off as nonchalant. "Just work, you know."

"No, Kady. I don't know, which is why I'm asking." He was well aware that she had to deal with a lot of bullshit from the men she worked with and competed against. The whole computer field—from programming to security to games— was male-dominated and somewhat proudly chauvinistic. Colton didn't agree with it in the slightest, but that didn't make it any less true. And for someone like *her*? Who was not only brilliant at the work but feminine and beautiful and sharp-tongued? Yeah, she dealt with more than her fair share of it.

"Bob was just worried about a meeting I had scheduled tomorrow, that's all," she said.

And now Colton was getting pissed for a new reason. Kady was lying to him. "Bob Chase is a tool," he said. "And he was hassling you about something over which you have no control, cutting you off, and generally, from what I could hear of your side of the conversation, being a pretentious, overbearing blowhard."

She shrugged again. "Pretty much. No biggie."

Except that wasn't true, either. Colton had known this woman for more than fifteen years. He knew her facial expressions, intonations, and body language—though, admittedly, not as well as he wished he could. And right now, the cast of her eyes, furrow of her brow, and curl of her shoulders all read that the call had upset her. And that combined with the fact that she wasn't being straight with him made him a little crazy. "Why did you go in the bathroom to finish the call?"

"Just trying not to disturb you," she said.

He stepped closer, so close they were almost touching. "You are so full of crap right now. You know that?"

Blowing out a breath, she retreated into the darkness of the small room and leaned her butt against the counter. Crossing her arms, she said, "Wow. You might want to brush up on how to win friends and influence people, Colton."

He hit the light and followed her into the space. "Don't deflect."

Her green eyes flashed at him. "Why are you pushing me on this right now?"

"Because I don't like to see someone I care about getting treated like shit, especially not by someone in a position of seniority at their job." *It sure as shit would never happen in my firm.* When she dropped her gaze to the floor, he bent down enough to force their eyes to meet. "How bad is it?"

"It's the same old BS. And nothing I can't handle." She looked to the side.

He caught her chin in his fingers and tilted her head to force her to look at him. "I know you can handle it, Kady. I just hate that you're in the position of having to in the first place." Maybe he could help. But how? A quick array of emotions flashed through her eyes. Colton frowned. "But why are you hiding it from me?"

"I'm not—"

He arched a brow, calling bullshit on her response before she'd fully voiced it. And the fact that she'd eaten the words proved he was right.

She gently wrapped her hand around his, gave it a squeeze, and pulled it away from her face. For a moment, Colton reveled in the warmth of her skin touching his even as his body registered the gentleness and was once again reminded of just why he could never have her the way he wanted. But if he couldn't have her in his bed and under his body, then he'd sure as hell do right by her *and* his best friend and protect her. Defend her. Stand up for her. Not because she needed him to do it. Not because she wasn't capable of doing it herself. But because it was the right thing to do.

And something deep down inside demanded it of him, too.

She dropped his hand and hugged herself again. "Look,

I'm going to say this, and you're not going to let it make things weird. Okay?"

A sliver of dread snaked around his spine. He nodded.

Kady heaved a deep breath, like she was bolstering her resolve. Then she met his eye. "You have looked at me as a little kid my whole life. And I get it. For a part of that time, I *was* a little kid. I'm six years younger and your best friend's little sister. When you were graduating college and entering the army, I was just learning to drive. By the time *I* was graduating college, you had a career and had fought in wars." She rubbed her hands over her biceps as if she were trying to warm herself. Colton jammed his hands in his pockets to keep from helping.

Between his ears, the horrible foot-in-mouth things he'd said to her that night in the pool house rattled around— words he'd said because he'd freaked out about the very things she was talking about right now. But the dismissive and insensitive load he'd dumped all over her that night had just been a pack of lies. Fact was, Colton had seen her go in the pool house moments before. He'd sought her out. And he'd known she'd had a crush on him for pretty much ever.

Thing was, by the time she'd hit her junior year of high school, he'd been crushing a little bit himself. His head saw the age difference, but his heart only saw someone who shared his interests, who could teach him things, and who made him *feel*. And the attraction only grew as he'd come home on leave and seen her, each time growing more and more into a woman. At his welcome-home party, she'd been beautiful and confident and so damn sexy that every rationale Colton had ever had for keeping his damn hands off had flown right out the window.

In truth, when he'd retreated from her that night after Tyler had interrupted what had been one of the hottest make-out sessions of his life—mostly because it involved the woman standing in front of him—Colton had been the one deflecting. Big time. Because his only other option was to give in to what he wanted.

Kady sighed. "I'm not that little kid anymore, Colton—"

"I know."

"Do you?" she asked, peering up at him. She blinked away and shook her head. "Our age difference isn't as meaningful as it was when we were younger, so I need you to see me as your peer, as your equal. Not as a little kid or a little sister who needs to be coddled or protected. I don't need you to worry about me or intercede in anything professional for me. In fact, if you ever did, it would just make things worse. In this field, I have to work twice as hard and be twice as creative to get half the respect. So I keep my complaints to myself and ignore as much of the bullshit as I can because otherwise it'll make me crazy and distract me from what's important, which is the work. Which I love. And I'm damn good at it, too."

"Yes, you are," he said without thinking. But some things were so true they didn't require thought. They just *were*. Anybody would be lucky to have Kady Dresco on their team, so Bob— His thoughts froze midstream. Anybody *would* be lucky to have Kady on their team...including him.

That thought was like a revelation, opening doors and windows inside his mind and making him wonder why the hell he'd never had this thought before. Because Kady would be an amazing partner—competent, brilliant, skilled, creative. She'd be the kind of person you could count on to get her shit done without needing oversight and to collaborate and brainstorm in a way that made everyone's work better. Exactly what he needed. Though, for sure, the idea of working with her wasn't without its complications.

Forcing away that question, Colton released a long breath. Not only was she right in this situation, she'd been right three years ago, too. He hadn't seen the real her. He hadn't seen a strong, independent woman. He did now, though. In spades. Damn if it didn't make her even more appealing.

"Okay. You're right. Though my gut instinct is to beat down any asshole who harasses you, I know you're tough enough to handle it and I'd never want to make things worse. But if you ever want my help—with anything—all you have to do is ask. And if you ever want to blow off steam, I'm here to listen." He pressed his lips into a line, hoping she wouldn't turn this into a joke per their norm, because this was important to him.

She stared at him as if evaluating his offer, and the seriousness in her expression mirrored what he felt in his gut. The pounding drumbeat of the rain on the roof above them drowned out all other sound, giving the moment an almost suspended quality. "Okay. I'll try," she finally said. "But I'm used to holding all this in, so it's not easy. I don't like to be seen as weak or incompetent."

Satisfaction roared through him at her serious reply. He felt like something important was happening here, something real, something—for once—not hidden behind layers of snark and humor. Colton didn't have anything real or even particularly meaningful with a woman—nor had he ever before. And that made what was happening between them right now stand out.

Not that he didn't have plenty of opportunities for casual encounters with women interested in dabbling in the rougher stuff with him, but none that made him want something more, something deeper, something *real*. Mostly, that was a good thing, because his parents' miserable marriage had seriously damaged his belief in the institution. His mother excelled in passive-aggressiveness and guilt trips, while his father was a master of actual aggression and yelling. Most of the time, they'd directed their venom at each other, but he and his sister Sophie had gotten caught in the cross fire plenty of times. Even after his parents had divorced and his father had moved to Tennessee, Colton had continued to get trapped in the middle of their disputes during the summers he spent there. If it hadn't been for his good friends Reed and Brock, those summers in Tennessee would've been miserable. So, Colton hadn't even been eighteen before he vowed he'd *never* spend even a minute as an adult putting himself in the situation he'd been forced to live through as a kid.

His gaze scanned over Kady's beautiful face. The woman standing in front of him was the *only* woman who'd ever inspired Colton to consider anything more than a one-night stand or being fuck buddies, and that made Kady both incredibly dangerous to his world order and one of the most important people in it.

"I don't see you that way. Not even a little," he said. Allowing himself the pleasure of her skin, he brushed his knuckles down her cheek. So fucking soft.

Her head tilted into his hand and she smirked up at him, one eyebrow arched.

"Okay, 'little' was a bad choice of words, wasn't it?" he

said, cupping her cheekbone in his palm and running his fingers into the edge of her hair.

She nodded, but the smile that played around her mouth made it clear she'd understood his intent. Licking her lips, she stared up at him.

Arousal shot like an arrow through Colton's body, spiking his pulse and sending blood south. As if Kady picked up on the shift in his mood, her lips parted and her skin flushed where he still held her. The air suddenly crackled with heat and tension and promise.

Colton's gaze zeroed in on her mouth, and an urgent need had him wanting—no, *needing*—to taste her. To claim her. To devour her. Without telling his body to move, he leaned down and his fingers slid into the silk of her hair. He met her gaze and he nearly roared in victory when she tilted her head back to receive him. Closer. And closer yet.

Her fingers fell on his lips. Her eyes bored into his, the beautiful green filled with desire and something else. Challenge? Determination?

"Don't do this unless you mean it, Colton," she said in a voice so low the beat of the rain nearly drowned it out.

The words pierced through his desire and kick-started the thinking part of his brain. *Unless you mean it.* Colton froze. What would "meaning it" mean to Kady? Something intentional. Something that might go somewhere. Something serious.

Regret and longing settled like an anvil on his shoulders. He slowly dropped his hand from her hair and pulled back. Need throbbed through his body, but his heart protested the lost promise of this moment even louder. Because he knew with Kady, sex would never just be about bodies and actions, it would be about feeling, connecting, sharing.

Kady was tough and brilliant, and she was also a happily-ever-after, two-point-four-kids, white-picket-fence kind of woman. Unlike his, her parents' marriage had been fantastic, and the Dresco house had served as a home away from home more than once for him and his sister Sophie. So Colton totally got why Kady would want the same. More than that, she deserved it. Which meant she deserved more than him.

"Like I said"—Kady's voice jolted him from his thoughts—"let's not let this conversation make things weird. Okay? I just needed to say that stuff."

He nodded. "Right. Of course," he said. Did she hear the grit in his voice? And what would she think it meant if she did?

She gave him a small smile and stepped around him, opening a clear path between him and his reflection.

Colton looked himself in the eye. *Could you give a relationship a meaningful try for her?* he asked his mirror image.

His gut gave a squeeze of alarm at the thought, not because of the idea of being with her, but because nothing he'd seen growing up had taught him how to be a good half of a whole. And he wouldn't be able to live with himself if he gave her anything less than the happy future she deserved.

And that wasn't the only question worth considering.

*Could you dial the roughness down for her?*

Another squeeze. Not really. He'd had "regular" sex before, and it could get him off. But no way he could *only* have regular sex. Something in him required the release of aggression that rough sex gave him. And for him, it was so much *more*…exciting, satisfying, fulfilling.

He couldn't change. Not this. And trying probably wouldn't serve his cause, either—instead, it was likely to create the same kind of tension and conflict that had cracked the foundation of his parents' marriage and slowly but surely rotted everything from the inside out.

If you couldn't be your true self with the person you planned to spend your whole life with, you shouldn't be with them in the first place.

Problem was, he cared about Kady Dresco—about what she needed and what she thought of him—too damn much to put their relationship at risk.

• • •

Kady busied herself with the ten new emails that had come in while she'd dealt with Bob and then Colton.

Colton. Who had almost kissed her.

Why the hell had he almost kissed her?

More importantly, why had she stopped him?

Kady's fingers pounded harder against the keyboard than perhaps was strictly necessary.

She knew exactly what she'd just missed. Colton Brooks kissed in an all-consuming way that stole her breath, demanded her surrender, and blocked everything else out until the only thing she saw or heard or felt or *knew* was his lips, his tongue, his hands, his body. *Him*. After all this time, she could still remember the almost aggressive way he kissed, claiming her with his mouth, his harsh grip, the hard press of his chest and hips and thighs against hers. Just the memory of it made her heart flutter.

And she'd just turned him down.

No, he'd just withdrawn. Again. Though, she respected him for being honest, at least, even if that led him to a different decision than the one she wanted. Much better than him taking advantage of her interest and willingness and putting them back in that awkward place they'd had to navigate after their ill-fated encounter at the party.

Which was exactly why she'd turned him down—or at least, made it clear what proceeding meant to her. Because as much as she'd seriously consider selling a kidney for one night of no-strings-attached sex with him—just *one*—she knew she wouldn't be able to weather the blow if he did anything that communicated that the fact he was with *her* wasn't important. And she suspected her ego might never recover if he pulled away midstream like he had the last time. It had taken Kady a lot of phone calls with Julie, who was hands-down the best listener among all her sorority sisters, long talks with her roommate Christine, quite a few pints of Ben & Jerry's, and therefore, lots of trips to the gym to make up for said emotional eating, to realize that what had happened between them that night had absolutely nothing to do with her.

But having worked so hard to achieve that insight, she wasn't putting it at risk again unless Colton actually saw her, actually wanted her, and actually intended to follow through. If she could put a check mark next to all three of those boxes, she would sign up for that ride in a heartbeat—and get on and off as many times as she could. Heh.

After their conversation, she felt better about the first of those. In fact, she almost felt like something had shifted between them. Maybe finally, after all these years, he'd truly realized she was an adult, a woman. Their near miss of a kiss proved he desired her, at least on some level. But the third?

Well, the fact that the kiss hadn't happened said it all.

Why did he find her so easy to resist? As much as she appreciated the honesty, she'd be lying to herself if she didn't admit to the ball of hurt feelings rolling around inside her chest.

Kady opened up a new email window and hammered out a thank-you message to Colonel Jepsen and his team. She smirked to herself as she typed the words "Thank you." Colton was *so* not winning that bet. She'd superglue her lips together before she let that happen.

"What did that keyboard ever do to you?" Colton asked from across the room.

Kady flinched and looked up to find him leaning against the wall outside the bathroom door like he'd been watching her. Heat bloomed over her skin. How long had he been there? And why was he looking at her?

*Maybe for the same reason he almost kissed you?*

*Ugh. Men are so freaking confusing. Especially that one.* "Uh, what are you talking about?" she said, gentling her keystrokes.

He grinned and shook his head. "Any chance you're getting hungry?"

Kady smiled. "I've been hungry since our driver mentioned the milk shakes."

"Wanna walk over and get some dinner?" Colton strolled toward the table.

"Yeah, sounds good." She hit send on her message, closed her laptop, and fished her phone charger out of her computer case on the floor. "And I'm even going to be a rebel and leave my phone here while it charges."

"Living on the edge," Colton said as he tugged on his shoes.

"That's me all right." Kady nudged her heels until they sat upright and stepped into them. The leather lining inside them was ice-cold from how wet they still were. Colton opened the door, letting in a wave of humid June air. "You know, I sorta can't believe we're going back out in this again. It's an actual monsoon."

Colton grinned and nodded. "True, but there was a big golf umbrella lying on the floor in the motel's office. I'll ask if we can borrow it. That'll help."

She stepped onto the narrow sidewalk and paused while he double-checked that the door was locked. "You know," she said over her shoulder as they made their way along the walkway, "if you just want to admit defeat on the whole me verbally expressing my gratitude thing"—she was careful not to use the actual words "thank you," because Colton was totally a strict constructionist when it came to the terms of a bet—"you can just buy me dinner now. I even promise to go easy on your wallet. I'll only order one milk shake and no dessert."

"Ha, just keep walking, Dresco. The night is still young."

Kady grinned. Well, if nothing else, at least their conversation now proved that their conversation from before hadn't made things weird.

At the end of the sidewalk, they dashed into the office. He held the door for her, and she slammed her lips shut as the words "thank you" nearly fell off the tip of her tongue. He smirked, then followed her in. "Mind if we borrow your umbrella to go to the diner?" Colton asked the man behind the counter.

"Not at all," the man said, dragging his gaze from his television program.

"Would you like us to bring you back anything?" Colton asked.

The old guy's eyes went wide and focused squarely on Colton. "I'd be much obliged for a cup of black coffee." He pulled out his wallet.

Colton waved him off. "Happy to. We shouldn't be too long."

"Thank ya, son."

Colton ducked his head and retrieved the big, colorful umbrella from a bucket in the corner.

"Aw, look at you being all sweet," Kady said under her breath as they paused at the door.

"Through and through, cupcake," he said with a wink.

She rolled her eyes, even though sometimes it was actually true. "Also, take note, that is the only time tonight you're going to hear those words."

For a moment, he frowned, and then she saw the light-bulb go on over his head. The old man had thanked him. "Keep talking smack and your loss is going to be that much more humiliating." He followed her out onto the sidewalk.

Kady looked at the kiddie-pool-size puddles covering every part of the parking lot's surface and stepped out of her heels. "I'll be more stable on bare feet," she said, her fingers hooked around the backs of the shoes.

"Don't know how much good this umbrella is going to do us," Colton said. "But it's better than nothing. Ready?"

Kady nodded.

The heat of Colton's arm slipped around her shoulders, sending a jolting thrill through her body. "Let's make a run for it," he said, raising the umbrella over them. "Stay close."

# Chapter Four

A little over an hour later, she and Colton had bellies full of burgers, fries, and Oreo cookie milk shakes and had delivered George, as he finally introduced himself, his coffee, as promised. The food had been good, the milk shake *amazing*, and their dinner conversation easy and flowing. And she'd caught herself twice before slipping and thanking him—once when he'd passed her the ketchup and again when he'd let her finish the last of his shake. They'd talked shop most of the time—sharing industry gossip and experiences with new software, speculating on the identity of a new hacker trying to make a name for himself, and other equally geektastic topics. Exactly the stuff she loved.

Kady didn't remember a time when she wasn't fascinated by computers, not just what they could do, but how they actually operated. She could still hear her mother's voice echoing off the walls of the family office totally flabbergasted that a nine-year-old Kady had disassembled the desktop PC.

When Kady managed to reassemble the machine so that it worked good as new, her father had found her some science and computer summer camps to apply to. By the time she'd turned ten, she'd known exactly what she wanted to do with her life.

She really loved that Colton got that about her. And he always had. Even when they'd bickered or harassed each other when they'd been younger, he'd always respected her interest and her ability. When they talked computers, he'd never cared that she was something of a nerd, nor did her being a girl seem to bother him.

Add all that together with the fact that the incredibly sexy man with whom she now found herself stranded had been an absolutely beautiful boy, and it was no surprise at all how hard she'd crushed on him.

The door to their room was barely closed behind her when Colton flopped on the bed and rubbed his stomach. "If I didn't think there was a serious chance of drowning out there, I'd go for a run."

Kady dropped her heels to the floor and her bare feet froze right where she stood on the industrial beige carpet. She barely heard his words because of the amount of brain capacity that had diverted to the visual he presented. One part of her brain—the biggest part, if she was going to be honest—focused on the fact that Colton's long, lean body looked so damn amazing all sprawled out on the bed that Kady wanted to pounce on him, especially since the way his left leg hung off the edge pulled his dress pants tighter across his groin, showing off the subtle but unmistakable outline of his cock. But another part—small but vocal—saw Colton lying on the bed and remembered that the room had only the one, and that they were going to have to share it.

As in, him and her, together, in *that* bed.

As in, her and the only man ever to give her an orgasm, together, in *that* bed.

Kady's stomach flipped as butterflies whipped through her middle. "Um, should we see if there's a movie on? Or something?"

"Why not?" Colton said, sitting up and raking his fingers through the chocolate brown of his hair. "I'm gonna get comfortable first, though."

Her gaze dragged to his dress shirt, still hanging on the back of one of the chairs. *That* was all she had for getting comfortable herself. "Yeah, might as well."

Colton grabbed a few things from his laptop bag and closed himself in the bathroom. When he came out a few minutes later, Kady couldn't help but gape.

"When did you get glasses?" she asked, knowing she was gawking at him but unable to help herself. Because as sexy as he'd been laid out on the bed, he was just as sexy wearing those dark frames. Damn, smart was sexy. And right now, Colton Brooks looked like a freaking genius.

"My last year in the army," he said in a tone that said he wasn't thrilled about it. "I usually only wear them at night, though. Otherwise, I wear my contacts."

"Oh," she said, a strange emotion she couldn't quite identify rolling through her in a long wave. Sadness. Because he'd worn contacts and glasses for *four* years and she hadn't even known. Something like that just felt like the kind of detail you should know about a friend. Though in fairness, before tonight she wouldn't have known exactly how to classify them. Sorta childhood friends through her brother, turned business rivals who had absolutely incendiary chemistry when they let it loose, which was almost never. Yeah, that wasn't unclear at all.

Sarcasm. Kady's second-favorite –asm.

"They look good on you," she said.

His eyebrow arched over one lens.

Annnd that was sexy, too. "What? I'm being serious." It was a testament to just how hot those damn glasses were that she was *just now* noticing that his pants hung loose on his hips as if he hadn't buttoned his fly.

"Well, thanks." He dropped a toothbrush and contact case into his bag.

"Ha," she said with a big smile. "You said it to me. That right there ought to earn me the win on this bet."

"If only that was the bet that we made. Which it wasn't." He stretched out on the bed again, and the position confirmed the accuracy of her suspicion about his pants. A good inch separated the button from its hole, and the top of the zipper was down. He was the devil. Really, he was. When he twisted to retrieve the remote control off the nightstand, the gap widened, flashing her a glimpse of black boxers.

White undershirt. Dark-framed glasses. Sneak peeks at black boxers. Really? How much more was a girl supposed to be able to take before she either spontaneously combusted or found a shower with a removable showerhead?

She scooped up her purse and Colton's shirt off the back of the chair. "See what's on while I change," she said. He nodded and started surfing channels, but she could've sworn she felt the heat of his gaze on her back.

In the bathroom, she quickly shed her blouse and bra and slid into the white cotton. And good God, it smelled like Colton. She pulled the collar to her nose and breathed him in. The masculine scent reached down into her belly and stirred things up until she found herself fantasizing about pressing her face, her nose, her tongue to his throat. For starters.

The thought had her glancing to the shower. No removable showerhead. The inhumanity.

Colton's dress shirt was so big on Kady that she had to roll up the sleeves twice just to free her hands. Despite the fact that the shirttail hung past her butt, she wasn't ready to walk out there with nothing between her and those glasses but the black satin bikini underwear she had on, so the skirt stayed, for now. Next, she brushed her teeth using the travel set she always kept in her purse—thank God—and brushed her hair, then she threw it up in a bun and stuck a pencil into it to keep it in place. She finished by washing her face and hands and refusing to give an ounce of thought to how Colton would think she looked.

They were just friends. It didn't matter.

"Find anything?" she asked as she walked out into the main room. She dropped her purse onto the chair where she'd been working and hung her blouse over the back. She'd have to travel in it tomorrow so she wanted it to be at least somewhat presentable.

"Come look," he said.

She turned and drank him in. Tight shirt. Glasses. Flash of boxers. Check, check, and check. Colton gestured toward the TV. Oh, right. Kady sat on the edge of the bed and kept her face forward so he couldn't see the blush that had to be filling her cheeks, if the rising heat there was any indication. Her inability to ignore her attraction to him clearly revealed a couple things, though. First, that she still found him incredibly appealing. Second, that she wasn't quite as over him as she'd told herself she was. And, third, that she was desperately in need of a good orgasm—and her body obviously recognized in him the one person guaranteed to make that happen.

"Let me know if something catches your eye," he said.

*Something has caught my eye, all right, but it isn't in that box on the other side of the room. Stop it, Kady!* She sighed. "Okay." Honestly, there wasn't much on that interested her, so before long her mind wandered to the book in her laptop case. She never traveled without reading material. Often, she read on an app on her phone, but she'd adored this particular story so much she'd bought the paperback, too.

It was an erotic romance—super dark—about an underground boxer who was shamelessly unself-conscious about the kind of sex he enjoyed—rough, *really* rough. The kind of sex that left fingerprint marks on arms and wrists, and bruises from pounding hip bones on the soft flesh of the thigh, and tenderness in the ass cheeks that made it hard to sit comfortably for days. The kind of sex that involved harsh words and hot taunts rasped in the ear, and the overpowering of the woman's body, and even role-playing involving force.

Kady had reread it so much that the pages fell open to her favorite scenes. Truth be told, she was shocked by how much the darkness thrilled her—so shocked she'd never even shared her growing interest and curiosity with her girls. But there was absolutely no denying it did. Maybe her interest in *this* explained her inability to orgasm with the men she'd dated. Maybe her experiences had all been too sweet and tender to get her there. Maybe it had nothing to do with Colton's wonder powers after all.

Thinking about the book made her yearn to build a little pillow fort against the headboard and curl up with it for a few hours, but no way she was reading that in front of Colton. For one thing, this book made her way too hot. For another, Colton would probably have the mother of all freak-outs if he knew that this was what turned her on. And if he ever told her brother? Oh, God. No. Nope. Not taking that chance.

"I don't really see anything," she said. "Do you?"

He shook his head, got up, and retrieved his laptop. "Netflix to the rescue," he said.

He lay down on his stomach and settled the computer at the top of the bed. As Kady shifted to stretch out next to him, she couldn't help taking a good, long look at Colton's ass. The looseness of his waistband had tugged the dark fabric down, exposing the dimples in his muscular lower back. God, he was a work of art. Really.

She lay down and tried not to think of her bedmate's well-sculpted butt.

"Oh, *here* we go," Colton said. "How about *Office Space*?"

"Oh my God, I love that movie." Kady grabbed a pillow, folded it in half and propped up her head so she could see the monitor. "I'm gonna need you to go ahead and come in tomorrow," she said, mimicking a line in the annoying supervisor's voice. "Mmkay? Oh, and I almost forgot, ahh, I'm also gonna need you to go ahead and come in on Sunday too, 'kay?"

Colton chuckled. "You clearly have excellent taste in movies."

"Th—" She swallowed the word.

His eyebrow arched. "Almost," he said in a low voice that

was way too damn sexy.

"Almost nothing," she said.

He smirked and clicked play, and they settled in as the credits started.

Soon, they were both laughing and saying some of the lines right alongside the movie and taking turns proclaiming their love for this scene or that. Really, you couldn't work in the computer field and not adore this movie's championing of the little-guy computer programmers' plan to swindle money from the evil firm so they'd never have to work again. It was damn near a cult classic.

As nice as sitting with Colton and working had been earlier, this was even nicer. Only rarely did she get to spend time with him when neither her brother nor their professional colleagues were around. And it gave her the opportunity all over again to admire his sharp sense of humor and revel in the sexy rumble of his laughter. All while he wore those glasses and lay two feet away from her on the bed.

Their room might've been old and out of style, but this night had turned into a little oasis of paradise in the middle of the Nevada desert. It kinda made Kady feel weird… sad?…that they would part ways again tomorrow afternoon. She mentally ran through her schedule for the next few months and couldn't readily determine when she'd next see him. And that sucked.

*Don't get attached, Kady.*

Right.

Except…

She couldn't actually think of a time when Colton Brooks hadn't owned a little piece of her heart. The admission set off a squeezing pang in her chest.

In the back of her mind, Kady could almost hear Regan telling her she was screwed.

When their first movie ended, it was still on the early side, so next they agreed on *The Matrix*, another movie with a computer programmer/hacker hero, this time set in the future. Kady readjusted her position, getting really tired of the confinement of her skirt, but still feeling strange about parading around in front of Colton in just her panties. "Mind if I get under the covers for this one?" she asked.

Colton's eyes flared. She could've sworn it. "'Course not," he said.

They got off the bed and folded back the bedspread and sheets, and Kady climbed in. Then she used the cover of the blankets to wiggle out of her skirt. She dropped it on the floor by the bed.

Colton still stood at the side of the bed, watching her.

Her whole body flashed hot. "What?"

He shook his head and lay down on top of the covers. "Nothing. Ready?"

When she nodded, he clicked play and the movie resumed.

She'd been all worried that sharing a bed with Colton would be awkward, but really, she was completely comfortable lying next to him. The only thing that would've made it better was if he reached over and tugged her into his chest. Though she was pretty sure that the contact of his cock against her ass—even through clothing—would probably make her spontaneously combust. So maybe the no-man's-land between them was for the best.

• • •

Colton was going out of his mind.

The woman of his fantasies lay on a bed next to him wearing *his* clothing. Every one of her throaty laughs reverberated down his body and settled a growing ache into his balls. Every little thing she did drove him crazy, from the way she twirled loose strands of hair from that appealingly messy bun around her finger to the way the slit in the back of that tight little black skirt taunted him with what lay beneath to the shapely curve of her calves whenever she bent her legs and crossed her ankles behind her.

And now the skirt was off. Jesus, when he'd realized what she'd been doing, it had taken everything he had to keep his feet planted where they were and not yank back the covers to help.

He still wanted to yank back those damn covers. He'd slide the pencil out of her hair and watch the black silk fall around her shoulders. And then he'd cover her body with his.

Colton heaved a breath and forced his mind to focus on the movie. With limited success at best.

Because, beyond the way her proximity tormented his body, he felt so damn comfortable hanging out with her that it was becoming disconcerting. He'd always known she shared his interest in all things computers and his appreciation for sarcasm, but spending this night with her also made it clear they clicked in other ways, too.

First, she was totally low maintenance. This whole day, she'd just gone with the flow, never complaining, never sulking, never taking the frustration of their situation out on anyone else. After eight years in the army, Colton knew the value of those qualities, because there were plenty of guys who'd spent all their time grousing about the heat or the sand or last-minute changes in orders. And they became as big a pain in the ass as whatever irritant had set them off in the first place. As far as Colton was concerned, life was too damn short to let every little bump in the road throw you for a loop.

Second, Kady had a fantastic sense of humor. He'd always known that to an extent, but all through the first movie, she'd done impressions and laughed until she snorted and never once seemed the least self-conscious about any of it. And it was so fucking sexy.

God, but every new revelation proved what an utter dickhead he'd been to her three years before. Because she'd been right. He hadn't really seen her then, but he sure as hell did now.

And Colton liked what he saw. A lot.

What the hell he did with that, though, he didn't have a clue. Liking and wanting Kady Dresco weren't the problems.

Next to him, Kady was fighting the lure of sleep. Her eyelids drooped and lifted, drooped and lifted, each time staying down just a little longer before she tried to pull herself back into consciousness. And then she was out. "Kady?" he whispered.

No response.

Though the movie still played, Colton's eyes remained on the woman lying next to him. They were both always so touchy around each other that he'd never before had a chance like this to just look at her. The way the waves of her hair curled around her face. The contrast between the shiny black and the pale porcelain of her skin. The pouty set of her lips and the little tilt of her nose.

She was cute and sweet and so damn gorgeous it was hard to take a deep breath.

But staring at her like this was absolutely pointless. He was just torturing himself with something he couldn't have.

Trying not to rock the bed, Colton rolled off his side and grabbed his laptop. Kady remained sound asleep, her lips parted and her face relaxed. Pausing the movie as he crossed the room, Colton settled the machine on the table and debated what to do. His internal clock said it was on the early side for sleeping, but he didn't want to disturb Kady, either. Might as well call it a night.

Rounding the table to double-check the door's lock, Colton's foot caught on something and he tripped. He bit back the curse sitting on the tip of his tongue and cut his gaze toward Kady. Still asleep. Turning, he found her laptop case lying flat on the floor, its contents half dumped out. He threw the dead bolt on the door, then knelt to put her things away.

Colton pushed a file folder, a notebook, and a few loose sheets of paper back into the bag, revealing a paperback with a dark-red cover. He flipped it over. And froze.

The image made him immediately hard. Or maybe it was that Kady owned a book with a cover that depicted a heavily muscled man holding a woman trapped against a wall, one hand binding both of hers above her head, the other resting on her collarbone *this close* from wrapping around the bottom of her throat. Only the placement of the man's forearm kept her breasts from being visible to the camera, otherwise the couple appeared nude. The woman's expression was part pain, part pleasure, and the man's was harsh, unforgiving. The book was called *Into the Dark*.

*What. The. Fuck.*

Peering over his shoulder to make sure Kady remained asleep, Colton flipped the book around in his hands and turned back to skim the description. The story was about an underground fighter who introduces a woman to the gritty worlds of his boxing circuit and of role-playing nonconsensual sexual scenarios.

Colton's heart was a pounding sledgehammer in his chest.

Why did Kady have this? Why was she reading this?

He turned the book over and over in his hands, taking in the curled cover, the bent corners of some of the pages, the cracked spine, an array of dings and scuffs and little tears. Signs of a well-read book.

And it was clear that certain pages were the most frequently read because of how the book was almost trained to open to them. Colton picked one toward the beginning and scanned his gaze over the words.

Holy shit.

He needed more light. And some privacy.

Turning out all the lamps in the bedroom to encourage Kady to stay asleep, he found the bathroom in the dark, quietly secured the door, and flicked on the light switch. He flipped the toilet lid down and sat.

Letting the book fall open by itself again, Colton started reading at the top of page sixty and couldn't tear his gaze away. It was all about the fighter trying to scare an interested woman away by coming on hard and strong. He'd tried to warn her away from him several times before, but since that hadn't worked, he was taking it up a notch. In the alley that led to one of the underground fight clubs, he got all in her space, barked questions and taunts at her, handled her roughly, and exposed her body by tugging her skirt up over her hips. When none of that seemed to chase her off, he yanked down her panties with a threat to fuck her right there in the alley where anyone coming to or leaving from the fight might see them. Imagine the guy's shock when he not only found her dripping wet but heard her beg him to do it.

Problem was, he liked the woman. He didn't want anyone else seeing her. And he wasn't convinced she understood that this behavior wasn't a game for him. It was who he was. What he did. What he *needed*. Instead, he roughly re-dressed her and handed her a card with an address. As he walked off, he challenged her to show up there in two nights, but only if she was sure she wanted and could handle the kind of sex he dished out.

Colton's hand was shaking as he turned the page.

*Kady Dresco reads books about rough sex.*

"Jesus," he whispered, the room spinning around him. He flipped a bunch of pages looking for the couple's next meeting, and finally just let the book fall open where it wanted. Annnd bingo.

He skimmed until he found the point at which the woman arrived at the address, found a note that said only "Come in" taped to the door, and entered the apartment. The lighting inside was dim and the place was quiet and still. She called out his name as she slowly moved around the space.

Out of nowhere, he was on her. He grabbed her from behind and hauled her tight up against the front of his body, one hand clamped over her mouth, the other strapped across her breasts and securing her arms.

*"Curious little thing, aren't you?"*

*Whimpering under his hand, she nodded, her heart racing and body vibrating with arousal. Four different times, he'd told her that she didn't want any part of what he had to offer. But when she was in his presence, she felt more alive than she had in years. The gritty rasp of his voice was like water, and the harsh press of his touch like air. Her body recognized in him something it needed very much, and she had to know one way or the other what he was, what he did, and whether she liked it.*

*"Do you understand what's about to happen here?" he asked, grinding his cock against her ass. "And I don't mean fucking. You walked through that door. That's a given." When she nodded again, he slid his hand from her mouth to her throat and said, "Tell me."*

*She swallowed hard and licked her lips. "You're going to be rough with me," she whispered.*

*His chuckle was hot in her ear and full of malice. "I'm going to be very rough with you. You can't handle it at any point, you say the word 'sunrise.' I'll stop immediately, and you'll walk out that door and never come back. Understand?"*

*Heat roared through her body. A slippery wetness already pooled between her legs and he'd barely touched her. "Yes."*

*Before the word was even fully formed, he shoved her forward, his grip still tight across her breasts, and pushed her down over the short end of the console table behind the living room couch. "Hands behind your back," he said, his hand anchoring itself around the back of her neck, forcing her chest and face against the cold, hard surface. He stood right in front of her face, which the height of the table perfectly aligned with his crotch. He undid his belt and tugged the buttons apart, baring his cock and letting it fall free against her cheek. "If you want it anywhere else, you'll take it here first. All of it."*

As his eyes scanned over the demanding blow job that followed, Colton tugged his fingers through his hair, his thoughts in an utter whirl of cognitive dissonance, his body so tight with arousal and need that it was nearly painful.

He sat reading Kady's apparent favorite scenes for so long that his butt fell asleep.

Every explanation he imagined for not just her possession of this kind of story but her obvious repeated reading of it seemed more impossible than the last. That she was just curious? Maybe. That she was fascinated by it? Possibly. That it turned her on and got her off? Boggle. That she wanted to try this for herself or already had someone who gave her this kind of sex?

Possessiveness and protectiveness roared through Colton's blood and hauled him onto his feet so he could pace the length of the small space. He held the book in a death grip until he finally dropped it to the counter. Bracing both hands against the edge, Colton leaned forward, dropped his head, and closed his eyes. His breathing was rough and he forced a deep in-and-out that failed to calm.

*Break it down, Colton. Right.*

On some level, Kady was interested in the kind of sex that was normal for Colton, the kind he never thought in a million years she'd go for. How interested was a complete unknown.

What else?

If she *was* actually interested, that removed a major fucking excuse he'd always had for keeping his hands off.

God knew he didn't want to corrupt her, scare her, or hurt her. Ever. But if this was her thing? That changed everything.

Didn't it? Or maybe not. Because it didn't alleviate his concerns about what Tyler would think if he ever learned what Colton was like. Granted, Colton wasn't a kiss-and-tell type of guy and these days, Tyler was often away saving the world one patient at a time, but that didn't mean he couldn't hear something through the grapevine.

Kady's interest also didn't resolve his concerns about where something between them might lead if he actually gave it a chance. He wouldn't want to lose her over a night of great sex, that was for damn sure. Which argued for giving something more real, more lasting a fair shake. But that required opening himself up to the possibility that an affair could turn into a relationship that would become *serious*. Could he deal with that? Because if he couldn't, then what this book meant to her should mean absolutely nothing to him.

Easier said than done. The thought of another man—any other man—roughing her up, holding her down, or fucking her until her legs could no longer bear her weight made him want to smash something with his bare hands. Repeatedly.

Hell, just imagining some other guy having sweet, tender, missionary sex with Kady Dresco made Colton's chest squeeze and gut sink.

Question was, what was he willing to do about any of it?

# Chapter Five

Kady woke up slowly. She was so comfortable that she didn't want to move. Her brain had a different idea, though, because it was immediately firing thoughts that tugged her into consciousness. Like, that she no longer heard the constant drumming of rain on the roof. Like, that she had no idea what time it was. Like, that she'd slept with Colton last night…and didn't remember a thing about it.

That one jolted her upright onto her elbows. Looking to her left, she found the other side of the bed empty. She frowned. The covers were all flat, like they'd never been rumpled because they'd never been slept under. Shifting into a sitting position, she gasped.

Colton sat staring at her from the chair in the corner, arms crossed over his chest, long legs out in front of him. He must've inserted his contacts, because he no longer wore his glasses. And sadly, he'd tucked his T-shirt back into his dress pants and secured them again. He looked gorgeous, but he didn't look happy.

"Hey," she said, shaking off the fog of sleep.

His eyebrows hitched and an unreadable expression passed over his face. "Hey," he said in a low voice.

She smoothed her hands over her hair. "It stopped raining?" He nodded. "What time is it?"

"Eight thirty," he said, his jaw ticking.

He was irritated with her. Why? What could she possibly have done? "Everything okay?" she asked.

"Just peachy, cupcake. Why don't you get dressed? You won the bet, so I owe you breakfast."

Kady's stomach squeezed and an icy dread slithered down her spine. Nothing about his tone or his eyes or his expression was playful. Normally, she'd be bragging about winning and he'd be doubling down on a new bet to regain the upper hand, but none of that seemed right with the way he was acting. "Uh, sure," she finally said. Sliding her legs off the bed, she ensured that his dress shirt covered her before she retrieved her skirt from the floor and stood. "Just give me a minute," she said as she scooped up her blouse and purse and made her way to the bathroom.

She freshened up and made herself presentable. Since he seemed to be in a rush for breakfast, she'd shower when they got back. When she was done, she gazed at her reflection in the mirror. Good enough.

Colton hadn't moved at all. Still just sat in that chair with that implacable look on his face. Finally, when she stepped into her still-damp heels, he pushed himself out of his seat, and that was when she noticed that he already wore his shoes, too.

Kady frowned. "Did you not sleep last night?"

Collecting the key chain from the little table, he shook his head. "Couldn't."

"I'm sorry. Was it me? Did I do something to disturb you?"

His eyes narrowed and his lips pinched. Just for a moment. And then his expression was neutral once more. "Just had a lot on my mind," he said.

Something was seriously wrong, but what could she do if he wouldn't open up about it? Regret and disappointment chased away her appetite. She really thought they'd connected and clicked yesterday, but he must not have felt it. "Okay. Well, maybe a yummy diner breakfast will help," she said, hoping to cheer him up and bring back even a little of the comfortable companionship and good times they'd had the night before.

He opened the room's door and gestured for her to go first.

When she stepped outside, the air was so humid it literally sat on Kady's skin. Dark clouds hung low in the sky as if the storm wasn't yet sure it was done. As they made their way to the diner, she sidestepped all the huge puddles that filled the low spots in the parking lot. Great lakes of water also sat on the road and on the scrubby field of grass on the other side of the street. What were the chances that the roads that led to the airport were clear with so much standing water everywhere here?

Yesterday, they'd run across this parking lot, Colton holding her tight against his side, the rain hitting them despite the big golf umbrella. They'd laughed and teased and had a good time. Now, the four feet between them felt like a world, as distant as he was being. Kady just didn't get it.

Inside, they joined about a half dozen other diners and

chose a table by the front window. Colton grabbed the plastic menus from behind the tiny jukebox and slid one her way.

"Thanks," she said.

He didn't even look up from his menu. She'd just thanked him and it didn't even seem to have registered.

"Any chance you're going to tell me what's bothering you?" she finally said.

His gaze cut to hers. "I told you."

"Mmkay. Have it your way."

The same waitress as last night, an older woman with big blond hair, brought them coffees without them even needing to ask. "What can I get for y'all this morning?"

"Some rye toast with butter and a fruit cup," Kady said, returning the menu to the rack behind the jukebox. She grabbed two packets of sugar for her coffee.

Colton frowned at her. "Thought you were getting the pancakes or Belgian waffle?"

Last night, she'd ticked off all the things she was going to order when she won the bet. But the weirdness between them had chased away most of her appetite and now she wasn't feeling particularly playful either. "I'm not hungry enough for all that," she said, nodding toward the waitress. "But you should order whatever you want."

"I'll take three eggs scrambled with white toast and home fries on the side," he said.

"You got it," the waitress said in a chipper voice. And then she was gone and they were alone again. Colton's gaze flickered from her to the tabletop to the window.

*Hello, awkwardness.*

How the heck did they get here after the awesomeness of yesterday? Kady was clueless. She sighed in relief when her fruit cup arrived in advance of everything else just because it gave her something to do. When the rest of the food came, they ate in silence.

Beckstein strolled in midway through their meal. He ordered at the counter, then did a double take when he saw them and headed their way.

Kady groaned. Bad enough to have to deal with Colton's silent treatment. She had no patience for Albert Beckstein right now. And hell, was he going to want to sit with them? She looked at the fork and debated jamming it in her eye.

"This looks cozy," he said.

Yeah, about as cozy as walking on crushed glass. His powers of perception were astounding. Truly. "And good morning to you, too, Al," Kady said as civilly as she could.

"So, uh, do you want to sit or something?" Colton asked.

Kady glared at him. He must *really* not want to talk to her if he wanted Beckstein to join them. For God's sake.

"Unlike some people, I have work to do. I'm getting takeout." He glanced over his shoulder to the counter. "Besides, I wouldn't want to interrupt."

Refusing to dignify the innuendo, Kady took a big overly crunching bite of her toast.

Colton placed his coffee cup down with a hard *clank*. "It's just breakfast between colleagues, Beckstein," Colton said. "Don't be an ass."

And that right there was the highlight of Kady's day so far and made her marginally less pissed at Colton for the way he was acting.

"Whatever," Beckstein said, turning on his heel and parking himself at one of the stools at the counter.

Kady's gaze stretched across the table. Maybe this would

finally thaw him.

"Ass," Colton muttered, then he took a big bite of scrambled eggs and focused on his food again.

Or maybe not. This morning was driving her batshit crazy. She peered up at Colton from under her lashes. The dark circles under his eyes did seem to support that he hadn't slept. But why?

Beckstein left carrying a big brown paper bag protectively against his chest. He very specifically reminded her of Gollum. Kady sighed.

Colton's phone buzzed and he fished it out of his pocket, making Kady realize she hadn't grabbed hers off the charger before they'd left. She'd been too damn distracted by Colton. But now he had something else to concentrate on besides his breakfast companion, and that irritated her even more.

When they were done eating, Kady was *done* dealing with...whatever this was. She fished a ten-dollar bill out of her wallet, slid it under the edge of her plate, and scooted out of the booth. "I have some work to do," she said.

Colton gaped up at her, and his gorgeous face just made her more angry. She didn't want to find him attractive right now because she was pissed at him. So she didn't give him time to respond before she turned on her heel, called a thank-you to the waitress, and pushed open the plate-glass door.

*Please, God, let me not run into Beckstein again.*

But as it turned out, she'd prayed for the wrong problem. The minute she laid eyes on the door to their room, she groaned out loud. Colton had the key. Perfect. Some dramatic exit this turned out to be. Maybe George had a spare. She'd made it almost all the way back down to the motel's office when Colton rounded the corner in front of her. "Key," he said, holding it up by the plastic tag.

"Yeah," she said, "I realized." She made an about-face on the sidewalk and swore she could feel Colton's gaze boring into the back of her head.

At the door, he paused and looked at her. "Breakfast was supposed to be on me."

Kady arched a brow. "Really? This is how you want to play this right now? You wanna talk about the bet?" It had been fun and playful and totally a *them* thing. But that was all over.

Colton stared down at her, his jaw ticking.

"Would you please let me in? I'd really like a shower and then I need to do some work."

Finally, he relented, and Kady beelined for the bathroom and locked herself in. She dragged out the shower for as long as she possibly could, dread pressing down on her shoulders and making her feel heavy and sluggish. It was going to be a very long day if Colton didn't snap out of whatever this was.

Soon, she was dressed in her blouse and skirt again, had put a little makeup on her face, and had blown her hair most of the way dry. At least she felt a little more human now.

Hand on the doorknob, Kady bolstered herself to deal with whatever was going on with Colton. She walked into the main room and found him sitting on the nearest corner of the bed, head down, elbows braced on his knees. He held something in his hands. A book, it looked like.

The walls sucked in on Kady and her pulse was an immediate roar in her ears.

Not just any book. *Her* book. Her absolute favorite erotic story.

• • •

"Promise me we can talk about this without things getting weird," Colton said, echoing her words from the day before. He'd spent half the night and all morning debating what the hell he wanted to do—what he *should* do—and it had left him feeling torn right down the middle. He wanted her, of that he had no doubt. But that didn't mean he was good for her. By the time she'd woken up this morning, he'd been exhausted and confused and pissed off. He'd just about reached the decision to sit tight and keep his mouth shut when she walked out on him at the diner—*and* paid for her own breakfast.

Both of those had stung hard and made him realize he was screwing up with her again. Big-time. And the only way to fix it was to lay it all on the line.

"You went through my stuff," she said, her deer-in-the-headlights gaze slowly shifting to outrage. Her cheeks nearly glowed they were so red.

He shook his head. "I didn't mean to. I tripped over the strap to your laptop bag last night and it spilled out." He held the book up between them. "Can you tell me about this, Kady?"

"Um, it's mine, and that's pretty much all you need to know," she said as she reached for it.

Colton yanked it away and rose to his feet. "I know that much—"

"You're being an ass right now. Give me the book," she said, marching up to him and planting her hands on her hips.

"I'm not trying to be. I'm trying to talk about something with you. Seriously." He nailed her with a stare. "Like we did yesterday."

Her eyes went wide and her whole face frowned. She

hugged herself. "Colton, I'm not talking about my sex life with you."

"Your sex life? So, you do this kind of stuff?" he asked, struggling to keep his voice even and to decide if he was thrilled at the possibility or terrified for her safety. It took so little to make this kind of kink go very wrong.

"What business of yours is it if I do?" she asked. "Let me answer that for you. None."

The lifelong friend and dominant male personality inside him both disagreed. "This kind of edgeplay can be dangerous—"

"Oh my God," she said, throwing up her hands. "Listen, *Dad*, thank you very much for the lecture on safe sex. It's just *maybe* possible that sometime in the last eight years of being an adult I've learned how to take care of myself." Her mouth dropped open. "Is *this* why you've been pissy all morning? It is, isn't it?" She raked her hands into her hair and tugged the length of it into a ponytail. "Because you don't approve, or, what? It offends you? *God*."

No, she had it all wrong. The irony. "Kady, that's not—"

"I'm so mad at you right now I can barely see straight," she said turning away and pacing toward the bathroom. "No matter what I do or don't do, you don't get to judge me." She whirled on him. "And if you tell Tyler about this, I swear I will never talk to you again."

As if he would. If he could just get a word in edgewise… "Kady—"

"Do you—"

"Kady!" he yelled, needing some way to get her attention, because now he was getting pissed off, too. She seriously thought he'd judge her? That he was some kind of judgmental asshole? He stalked up to her and essentially trapped her against the closet doors. Heaving a deep breath, he muscled the anger back. That wasn't going to help anything. Besides, weren't her worries about his reaction similar to the ones he feared about hers?

*Aw, hell.*

"I'm not judging you and of course I won't tell Tyler." Skepticism filled her gaze. He shook his head and couldn't help the humorless laugh he chuffed out.

"This isn't funny," she said, crossing her arms.

"No, it's not. It's serious. I'm trying to be serious."

"Right. It's dangerous. Message received."

Goddamnit, she had a smart mouth on her. *So many* things he'd like to do to temporarily cure her of that. And now he knew she'd enjoy them, too. "Kady, I just meant—"

She huffed, stoking both the flames of his aggression and his arousal. "I got it."

He fisted his hands. "No, you fucking don't, because you won't stop talking long enough for me to explain myself."

She blanched. "Well, do it. What do you want to say?"

Here it was. Moment of truth time. Fucking finally. "Three years ago—"

"Colton, I don't want to talk about ancient—"

He was on her in a flash. One hand over her mouth, the other cradling the back of her head so that he didn't hurt her when he shoved her against the closet door. He held her there with the weight of his own body, his legs on the outsides of hers effectively boxing her in. "It's not your turn to talk. Understand?"

Eyes wide, nostrils flaring, Kady searched his eyes and finally nodded. He could almost feel the questions rolling off of her.

"*Three years ago*," he said again, arching a brow, "I pulled back from what we started for a couple of reasons. Same reasons why I pulled away again yesterday when I wanted to kiss you. But this book…this book makes me wonder if maybe one of those reasons isn't as relevant as I originally thought." He heaved a breath and leaned his forehead against hers, bringing them eye to eye. "The guy in your book? *I'm that guy*," he said, putting it in terms he hoped she'd understand.

A shiver ran over her body. Against his chest, her nipples went hard.

Holy hell. Did his declaration just turn her on?

Her pupils were dilating. Right there was his answer. His cock went from hard to downright torture.

"You get what I'm saying?" he asked. A small nod. "I get off on being rough. Because I like and respect you, *and* because you're my best friend's little sister — "

Her brows furrowed.

He pressed his hand more firmly against her mouth and nailed her with a stare. "I get it. After our talk yesterday, that's not how I see you. But it *is* how Tyler sees you. How he'll *always* see you. Big brothers are genetically programmed to be protective of younger sisters no matter their age. Trust me. I know from firsthand experience. So I've backed off because I didn't want to scare you or offend you with what I want, and I certainly didn't want to piss Tyler off, either."

Her fingers pulled softly at the hand covering her mouth, a gentle plea. He removed his hand immediately. "Can I say something now?" she asked quietly.

When had Kady Dresco *ever* asked for permission to speak around him? But he'd exerted a little dominance over her, and she'd responded with submissiveness. Probably wasn't even aware she'd done it. A dark satisfaction heated his blood and further hardened his cock. "Go ahead."

"I've never done any of the stuff in that book," she said, her voice breathy. Colton's gut dropped to the floor. Had he just read this thing all wrong? "But I want to. I've wanted to for a while. It's just really awkward to ask a man to rough you up during sex. It either leads to them thinking you're a wack job or it ends up feeling really cheesy." Her cheeks pinkened as she spoke.

That was because she hadn't been with a man for whom dominance was in his blood. "Why do you want to?"

"Um." She ducked her face.

Colton caught her chin in his fingers and forced her to meet his gaze. He was so close to her truth he could almost taste it. "Why?"

She swallowed hard. "Because I, um, can't…" She shook her head. "It's the only thing that turns me on."

*Good answer.* God, his mind was blown here, but she really did seem to have an interest in the same kinks he enjoyed. Which made her his absolute perfect match. They were like flip sides of the same coin. "I understand that completely," he said. "Because I'm the same way. But what is it you can't do? What were you about to say?"

She dropped her gaze.

"Kady," he said in a stern voice.

Her eyes rose to his. "I can't come. With a man."

Colton frowned. "You came with me." Of that he had no doubt, since he'd had his hands and mouth on her when it had happened both times.

"Yes," she said, licking her lips.

"So…" Confusion gave way to clarity. "Wait, are you saying I'm the only man—"

"If you crack a joke right now I swear I will knee you in the junk."

A dark, possessive satisfaction rose up within him. She'd only ever come for him? No other man? He probably shouldn't like that as much as he did, but he fucking loved it. "No jokes, I promise. Can you come…on your own?" he asked, hearing the arousal coloring his voice.

She nodded. "Why do you want to know this stuff, though?"

Was that hope in her tone?

Time to make a leap of faith—and hope she leaped with him. "I want you, Kady. I've wanted you for *years*. I've gotta be honest and tell you, though, that the idea of long-term relationships freaks me out. The disaster of my parents' marriage has made me gun-shy. But you're the only person who's ever made me want to try, and the fact that you like what I like? Every part of me is saying to grab on to you and hold you tight. I know this is sudden, but I can't help it."

Her mouth dropped open and her chest rose and fell faster. "Wow. Okay. I think…I can't…I might be having an out-of-body experience right now. I feel like I have wanted you my entire life, but I always knew you didn't want me. Hearing you say all this is kinda shaking the ground beneath my feet."

Colton's heart thundered in his chest. "In a good way, I hope?"

"In the best way," she whispered.

"Then it all comes down to this. What do you want, Kady?"

# Chapter Six

Kady's heart was beating so hard and so fast that she was dizzy and breathless. Or maybe that was from Colton covering her mouth with his hand as he slammed her up against the wall. Holy crap, but she'd never gotten so wet so fast in her entire life.

Self-preservation kept trying to say this couldn't be happening. She couldn't be finding out that the man of her dreams—literally—had finally decided he wanted her *and* he was ready to follow through and truly give them a chance *and* he was totally into the same kinky stuff she was. It was like the rarest alignment of the planets happening right when she needed it most.

"You," she said, answering his question. "I want you. I've wanted you since I was old enough to have those kinds of feelings."

He tilted his hips into her belly, grinding his cock against her. That her desire turned him on was just a freaking thrill.

"The rough sex. You understand that's not a game for me? It's not something I turn on and off? It's just how I am? You understand all that?"

Kady was shaking so hard she suspected the press of Colton's body against hers was more responsible for holding her upright than her own legs. "Yes, I understand."

"Anything you don't want or don't like?" he asked, his mouth nearly touching hers.

She needed to kiss him so bad. She tipped her mouth to his.

His hand caught her jaw in a steel grip, his fingers pressing into her cheek and neck, the pressure of his thumb forcing her mouth open. "Answer me, Kady. It's important."

Thank God, this moment wasn't the first time she'd ever thought about his question. From so much reading and some occasional porn viewing, Kady felt like she had a pretty good handle on what turned her on and off. "I don't want to be hit in the face. I don't want anything that will leave a mark somewhere clothing couldn't hide." His lips caressed the corner of her mouth, her cheek, the soft spot in front of her ear. Kady shuddered. "I don't want anything that could permanently damage my skin."

"Good, good. Anything else?" he asked, his lips pressed right against her ear. His tongue snaked out to lick and tease her there.

"Not that I know of, but can I say if I don't like something?"

He reared back and looked her in the eye, his expression serious. "Always. In fact, I have to demand it. Never let yourself be physically harmed or emotionally distressed."

Kady nodded, reassured by the way he was trying to learn about her and absolutely amazed that this was *Colton* she was talking to. She'd always known he was bossy and sometimes controlling, but she never would've guessed in a million years that *this man* lay beneath the surface of the one she'd known all these years. Then again, he hadn't known it about her, either.

"How about…hair pulling?" he asked, his hand sliding into her hair and loosely grabbing a fistful.

The spike in her pulse answered first. "Yes."

His fist tightened and yanked her head backward, opening her neck to his lips. Kady moaned.

"Spanking?" he asked, his other hand roughly sliding down her body until his hand landed on her ass.

"Yes," she rasped.

He squeezed and kneaded at her cheeks through her skirt. "Deep-throating?"

The face-fucking scene from her book came immediately to mind. "Yes." She pressed her lips to *his* ear this time. "I have a very tolerant gag reflex."

"Jesus," he bit out. "Being restrained?"

"Please," she said, trembling with need against him and remembering the way he'd pinned her hands above her head all those years ago. His hand pulled her hair harder, bowing her whole body, allowing him to kiss and lick and nibble down her throat to her chest.

"How about my hands on your neck?" He lightly bit the side of her neck, causing chills to break out all over her body.

This one was harder to admit, but reading about it or seeing it done always made her body crazy. "I want to try it," she said.

"We'll go slow," he said. "Last one. How 'bout anal play?"

This totally fascinated her, too, but she was more scared

of it. "Maybe. It scares me."

"Okay," he said with a nod. "And I'm really fucking proud of you for being so open with me." His eyes found hers and Kady melted at the arousal and affection she saw there.

Finally, he kissed her. Using his grip on her hair to guide her position, he grasped her jaw with his other hand and absolutely devoured her in a breath-stealing, bone-melting, soul-stirring kiss. Kady whimpered and moaned and clawed at his hair to try to pull him closer. She was possibly as close to an orgasm as she'd ever been without any stimulation to her clit.

Colton ground his cock against her belly until Kady was literally panting and dripping for him. Her panties were uncomfortably damp between her legs. When he abruptly broke off the kiss, she whined.

He grinned darkly. "Just one other thing. We need words. A slow-down word in case you need me to back off. And a safe word that will stop everything. I propose 'sunshine' for the safe word. What do you think?"

Kady smiled as heat filled her cheeks. "Yeah, I like that."

"Everything we're talking about, and you blush when I reference your book," he said, running his knuckles over her cheek. "So damn pretty. How about 'monsoon' to slow things down? Would those work for you?"

"Look at you being all sentimental," she said. But she actually loved it. She knew from her reading that the words were supposed to be things you wouldn't normally say so as not to accidentally blurt them out and interrupt what was happening. But these words did the double duty of also reminding them of this place, this weekend, this moment.

He smiled and winked. "I think this occasion warrants it, don't you?"

"Yeah," she said with a smile of her own, really loving having sweet, playful Colton back again. "I really do."

"So what are your words?" he asked, looking her in the eye.

"'Monsoon' asks you to slow down or back off. And 'sunshine' makes everything stop if there's a problem."

"Good," he said, his expression satisfied and eager. "Any other questions?"

She shook her head, lust-drenched dizziness threatening.

He arched a brow. "You sure? Because once we start I am going to be *all* over you."

*Yes, please!* "I'm sure," she managed.

"Good. Then that's enough talking for now."

Kady's heartbeat tripped into a sprint. She wasn't exactly sure what she was supposed to do, but her instinct said to try to get away from him. To play the kind of games she loved in her books. In the book he'd just read. She pressed her back up against the closet and dragged herself out of his hold.

The satisfaction and challenge that slid into Colton's expression spiked arousal and heightened her confidence. Slowly stepping around him like he could strike at any moment, Kady gave him a wide berth, then suddenly bolted to the left, past the bathroom door and into the bedroom. Running as fast as she could in her heels, she beelined for the door. Exhilaration shot through her as she heard him give chase.

Her hand just twisted the knob when his reached over her shoulder and held the door closed. A split second behind, his body collided with hers and trapped her against the cold metal.

He quickly threw the dead bolt and kissed the back of her neck. "Where do you think you're going?" he growled and rubbed the bulge of his cock against her ass. "God, Kady, that you're willing to play with me like this makes me so hard."

She moaned at the feel of his body and the urgent need in his voice. "Colton," she whispered.

He forced her to turn around.

With precision flicks of his fingers, he unbuttoned her blouse and pushed it down her arms, then made quick work of her bra.

"So pretty," he whispered as he leaned down and fondled and kissed her breasts. First one, then the other. When he sucked a nipple into his mouth and flicked it with his tongue, she unleashed a needful cry. "Like that, don't you?"

"Yes," she whispered.

For long minutes, he worshipped and tortured her breasts until Kady thought her body might melt. "Let's see what else you like. On your knees," he said, pressing on her shoulders and urging her down.

Kady sank to the floor, her body wedged between his muscular thighs and the motel room door. A sharp thrill made her stomach feel like she'd crested the highest hill on a roller coaster. Despite that incredibly hot night three years ago, she'd never before seen Colton's cock. She could barely breathe for the anticipation of seeing him, touching him, sucking him.

"Take me out and taste me," he said.

*Oh, yes.* The commands were like little shots of aphrodisiac, each one causing a slow burn on its own, but together, able to ignite something absolutely incendiary. She squeezed her thighs together to provide some friction for her aching clit as she unfastened his dress pants and pulled them and his boxers down far enough to free him.

Nearly panting, she took him in hand. Colton's groan was the sweetest victory. He was hot and thick and long and she reveled in the lubrication that his own pre-come provided as she wrapped her fingers around him and stroked him. Leaning forward, she swirled her tongue around his head before finally sucking him in.

"Such a hot little mouth." His fingers plowed into her hair and held the back of her head. He didn't force her, but the threat of it was there. Instead, he gave her time to learn him, explore him, find a rhythm that combined her hands and mouth. Little groans and gritty curses spilled out of him, and Kady would've sucked him off all day just to hear the sounds he made. "Take it slower, deeper."

Gripping his thighs with her hands, she inhaled a deep breath, and pushed her face forward into his groin as far as she could.

Colton grabbed her by the back of the head and the jaw, taking control of her movement and filling her throat with his cock. "Oh, God. Hold it, hold it, hold it. Yes." He released her and Kady gasped for air. "Again," he ground out, and she impaled her mouth on his cock, her lips wrapped around the base, and fought the instinct to pull back. "That's a fucking hungry little mouth, isn't it? Look at me."

Tilting her head as much as she could with her mouth full of him, she met his gaze. Dark eyes on fire, mouth open, chest heaving. He was fucking gorgeous.

"Yeah. So hungry for me. Aren't you?" He withdrew.

"Answer me."

"Yes," she said, peering up at him and panting for breath.

Masculine satisfaction slid into his gaze. "Tell me you want my cock."

Was this really happening right now? Was this really her Colton? Because she absolutely loved it, loved…him? "I do, I want it."

"I know you do. Open," he said, one hand grasping her hair and the other hand pulling down her jaw. And then his cock slid across her tongue. In and out. Slow and gentle at first. "God, I have thought about this so many times."

Kady moaned in response, half wishing she could get free long enough to tell him she had, too.

"Hold on, now." His hips really started to move, and Kady barely had time to brace on his thighs. He bottomed out in her throat again and again, putting her tolerance to the test. "So fucking good," he growled. Pressing her head backward into the door, Kady surrendered to the demands of his thrusts, loving the feel and the weight and the taste of him.

He pulled away abruptly, then slid his hands under her arms and lifted her to her feet. His tongue filled her mouth a moment later as he boxed her against the door with his body. Harsh hands ran down her breasts and stomach to her hips and worked her skirt upward until her panties were fully exposed.

"These clothes are going to smell like me for however long you have to wear them," he said around the edge of the kiss. He pushed her panties down over her hips, and she shimmied until they fell down around her ankles.

While Colton remained clothed from head to toe, Kady

stood trapped against the door, nearly naked. She moaned, a thousand percent ready to beg for an orgasm as soon as her mouth was free. Her fingers dug into his shoulders and her thighs actually trembled from the depth of her need. "Colton, please," she rasped.

"That's right. Beg me. What do you want?" His fingers raked over her thighs—the outsides, the front, the front center.

"Oh, God," she moaned as his tongue invaded her mouth again, making it hard to think. She shifted her hips, trying to make him touch her where she needed.

Hard hands clamped down on her ass. "Be still or I won't let you come."

"Colton," she whimpered.

"I could fucking live on the need I hear in your voice right now."

"*Please*," Kady whimpered, more desperate for this than she'd ever been for anything in her life.

Colton kicked her feet apart, slid his fingers through her wet, slick folds, and plunged two fingers in deep. The penetration combined with the friction against her clit made her come on contact. Kady screamed and her vision blurred and she sagged against Colton so completely that he had to hold her up.

"Yes. Yesyesyes," she moaned as he curled his fingers against the front wall of her core and fucked her in a short, fast rhythm that kept his thick fingertips in constant contact with an excruciatingly sensitive area inside her.

"You aren't getting my cock until you come again. I want you to come so hard my whole hand is wet with it."

"Colton, I can't. I can't." She was almost sobbing from

the pleasure and the intensity that nearly turned it to pain.

He braced his hand on the door above her shoulder and nailed her with a hot, intense stare. "Oh, you sure fucking can. Wait for it." He worked his hand harder, shifting from an in-out to a front-to-back rhythm which targeted that sensitive spot. The movement of his hand made her wetter and wetter, until she could *hear* just how wet she was.

An immense, pleasurable pressure built up around his fingers until she knew that she was not only going to come but that she was going to soak his hand, just as he'd demanded. She grabbed on to his arm, needing something to hold, something to anchor her against the wave of sensation building inside her.

"That's right, sweetheart," he rasped.

Holy shit, she was gonna— "Colton!" she screamed.

"Yeah. There it is," he gritted out, his hand still moving, drawing her orgasm out until it was almost painful. "You just came all over me. Taste." He pushed shiny, wet fingers into her mouth.

She grasped his wrist and sucked him in to the knuckle. In the wake of the two massive orgasms he'd just given her, she was so filled with gratitude that she would've gladly done anything he asked. Even as good as her own orgasms could be, there was simply no comparison. She'd never really thought she'd been lonely the past three years until this very moment. Now? Absolutely. How was she going to go back to the way things were after *this*?

Colton's hand cupped her face as he pulled his fingers free of her mouth. He bent down to align his eyes with hers. "Everything okay?" he asked.

The emergence of sweet Colton brought the sting of

tears to the backs of her eyes. Here he was, taking care of her in yet another way. "Everything's perfect," she said.

A small, tender smile played around his lips for a moment, and then it dropped and his eyes went molten. "Good, then bend over the damn bed."

• • •

Colton watched Kady, waiting to see what she would do, how she would react. Because she'd surprised him over and over. Even when he'd guessed correctly what her reaction might be, he'd had absolutely no idea what it would feel like to be doing any of this with her.

Kady blew every one of his fantasies entirely out of the water. Brave, daring, willing to give herself over to the daring pursuit of absolute abandon, he found her appealing in ways he never even knew to imagine.

She'd talked about wanting him to see her. Well, today, right now? He realized how damned much he'd been wanting—no, needing—someone to see him, too. See him and accept him for everything that he was. And not just someone. Her. Kady.

And, damnit, she *got* him. He could see it in her eyes, hear it in her voice, feel it in her touch.

Kady's eyes darted to the side, and Colton smiled inwardly. She was thinking about running again. *Do it, Kady. I dare you.* "Keep me waiting one more second and I'm going to make you sorry." When she still didn't move, Colton grabbed her arm and dragged her stumbling toward the bed. He'd been keeping an eye on her throughout this whole thing—a very close eye—and everything he saw told him that what they were doing turned her on and got her off.

Damnit all to hell, but Kady Dresco was perfect for him in every way—including her smart mouth—and she'd been right in front of him all this time. Realization and certainty crashed into him—he'd never find someone better suited to him. And he didn't even want to look.

Colton was caught up deep enough in his thoughts that when he released her and shoved her onto the mattress, he wasn't prepared for her to use the momentum of his push to scrabble across the bed.

She tossed him a challenging glance as she bolted off the other side, smiling and laughing.

Colton felt the grin crawl up his face. Damn if he didn't love her playfulness. "Aw, you are going to pay for that." He shot around the bottom of the bed and took off after her. He easily caught up as she dashed into the bathroom, then stalked her until her sweet little ass came up against the countertop.

"Sorry, sorry," she said, smiling and shaking her head and trying to flatten herself against the tile.

"Too late for that," he said, still wearing that grin. "See, I was going to give you the soft warmth of the bed, but maybe this suits you more." He claimed her mouth in a hard kiss. Kady literally melted into him and moaned like he was the water she needed to drink.

Her hands wrapped around the back of his neck and slid into his hair, tugging and pulling and scratching in a way that drove him wild. She wrenched her mouth away. "*Please*."

"I like it when you beg." He whirled her around, tore off his T-shirt, and pushed her upper body forward until she hovered over the counter. Frustrated by the clothing that separated them, he undid his pants and shoved everything down around his thighs. Then he caught her by the arms. "Want to watch me fuck you?" he asked, his blood scalding hot with the need to bury himself deep.

Kady bit down on her lip and nodded. "I'd love that."

That made two of them. But Colton was also very conscious that this was their first time together. Even though they were playing and he knew she was completely into it, he couldn't be rough about this moment.

Taking himself in hand, he aligned his head with her opening—

He wrenched back. "Goddamnit. Let me get a condom."

Kady blinked as if pulling herself from a fog. "I'm on birth control," she said. "And I'm healthy."

Going bareback inside her was a fucking dream he never thought he'd experience. "I'm clean, too, Kady. But are you sure?"

She nodded. "I trust you. Now, please."

Satisfaction roared through him. He tugged her upward so he could speak right into her ear and met her gaze in the mirror. "Tell me you want me inside you, Kady. Tell me you want me so deep I might never find my way back out again." Intense pressure bloomed inside his chest. He was well aware he was asking for more than her confirmation that she wanted his cock.

She leaned her cheek against his. "I do, Colton. I want you inside me. I want you *everywhere*." Maybe it was wishful thinking, but the look on her beautiful face told him her answer was bigger than just this moment, too.

And it was all he needed to hear. Still holding her arms behind her back, Colton bent his knees, tilted her hips, and slid his cock into her tight, wet heat. "Fuck, you are so small. Don't let me hurt you," he growled.

"You won't." She moaned and bore down on him, taking him in deeper.

Colton wanted to hold back, to resist, but she was too damn hot and wet and *good*. And his need for her could only be denied so long. He bottomed out inside her, his balls settling against her sensitive flesh. "That's a good girl, taking all of my cock." He bit down on the soft tendon that ran between her neck and her shoulder. Against his stomach, her hands fisted and unfisted, her nails scratching his skin.

"Please, please move. God, you have to move." Molten green eyes pleaded with him in the mirror. Her hips wiggled and tried to make him.

Colton groaned. "Oh, yeah, Kady. You fuck me." He loosened his grip so she could move. Because of the way he restrained her arms, she could only do so a little, and her growing frustration reached between his legs and squeezed his balls. He let her struggle for another moment and then tugged her back against him. "What do you want?"

"*You.*"

Colton held himself still, hand around her throat—an excruciating feat of discipline. His cock absolutely throbbed for the need to move. "Give me the words and tell me what you want me to do."

A flush ran over her chin from her cheeks down her neck to her chest, where the luscious mounds of her breasts jutted out from her position. "Fuck me. I want you to fuck me."

His cock jerked inside her. "How do you want it?"

"However you want to give it to me," she rushed out.

Colton gave a satisfied chuckle. "Brace your arms on the counter."

Kady moved like her life depended on it, and her urgent need escalated his.

Grasping her hips, he withdrew almost all the way to the tip and then slid all the way in again, a soft, teasing stroke just to allow them to get the feel of each other. The next stroke was just as slow on the withdrawal, but he snapped his hips and drove back in, shoving her whole body forward. More of those hard, punctuated thrusts followed, knocking a moan out of her every time.

It was all the adjustment he could allow her before the heat in his head and his chest and his gut demanded total abandon. Colton grabbed her hips and fucked her hard and fast. Her rhythmic moans turned constant at the harsh pace. Wanting her absolutely wild, he angled his thrusts to hit her G-spot. Now that he knew she was capable of coming so forcefully, he wanted her doing it on him again and again. With his other hand, he reached around and massaged her breast and pinched and rolled her nipple. And then he wrenched her up into an almost-standing position, one hand across her breasts, the other dragging down to find her clit. He circled his fingers there and she screamed.

Her orgasm fisted at his cock and her slick wetness coated him. "Fuck, yeah," he roared, fighting back his own release. He wasn't done with her. Not by a long shot.

"Oh, God, Colton," she said in a low, wrung-out voice.

"I want you under me," he said as he pulled out and kicked his pants off the rest of the way. He turned her around, then he lifted her into a fireman's carry over his shoulder.

She let out an indignant cry and beat at his back. "Put

me down!"

Colton chuckled and swatted her on the ass. Kady screamed and laughed as he threw her onto the bed and crawled up over her, his hips and legs pinning hers, his hands manacles around her wrists. "You're mine." He grasped his cock, forced her thighs apart, and slid home again. "This body. This pussy. *Mine*."

"Yes, yes," she said, her mouth dropping open and her eyes closing.

"Tell me, Kady. Mean it." Still holding her wrists, he fucked her in an alternating pattern of fast and shallow and slow and deep.

"I'm yours, Colton. Make me yours." She lifted her head, seeking a kiss, and he was only too happy to give her what she wanted. It was rough and possessive and fucking delicious.

Halting his movement when he was buried deep, Colton pushed her legs down straight and carefully slid his thighs on the outside of hers. The length of his cock kept him inside her even with her hips forced flat by the position, which ensured that he rolled over her no doubt over-sensitized clit with every stroke. He pushed her arms up straight above her head and held her there, completely flat and trapped beneath him. Damn, this was where he wanted her to stay forever.

"Oh my God," she moaned when he started to move, making sure to grind against her with every thrust. Sex filled the air, their scent, the wet sound of their fucking, the slap of skin on skin, and harsh, panting breaths.

Slamming his hips down on hers, he knew he was probably going to bruise her with his hip bones, and he fucking loved the idea that she'd wear him on her skin, too. That days later, she'd see the evidence of their lovemaking and think of *him*.

Lovemaking. Was that were they were doing? *You really have to ask that, Colton?*

No. Not really.

And that realization shoved him hard toward his orgasm. He released her arms and curled his hands around the top of her head, giving him leverage to drive into her hard and fast. Her arms came around him, gripping and clawing and holding him. Damn, how he hoped she marked him, too.

Hunching himself around her, Colton kissed her with his eyes wide open. She did the same, seeming to understand his unspoken command. They sucked and licked and bit at each other as he fucked her. "You're going to make me come. Where do you want it?" he asked.

Her hands slid down and squeezed his ass. "Inside. Don't leave me."

The words kicked him in the spine and had him driving into her. If he was going to come in her, he was going to be as deep as possible. In a fast motion, he slid his knees between hers again and lifted her legs up so high she was nearly bent in half. One arm holding her leg, he braced his weight on the other against her collarbone. "Here it comes," he rasped, feeling her swallow beneath his hand.

On his second thrust, Kady came. Her face crumpled in pleasure and her pussy went painfully tight and maddeningly wet around his cock.

Colton's orgasm plowed through him and he jerked and poured himself inside her. "Fuck, Kady," he growled, moving helplessly through the almost-violent release.

The minute it was over, the haze of aggression fled from Colton's mind. It was always that way, as if a pressure valve had been opened and drained. Until the next time.

He kissed her once, twice, gently and reverently. The smile of satisfaction she wore reached through his sternum and grasped his heart.

Easing up off of her, Colton slowly withdrew as a rock took up residence in his gut. He didn't want this to be the only time. He didn't want this to end at all. Rubbing her hip, he said, "Stay right here for a minute." He slipped off the bed.

Staring into the bathroom mirror as he waited for the water to warm, Colton's mind churned. He wasn't sure what to do or where they went from here. Even aside from the bullshit in his head, there were logistics to consider. They had jobs and houses in two different places. Could they do a long-distance relationship? Probably. Did he want to? Not at all.

So then, what was his plan?

# Chapter Seven

Kady could barely move, and she'd never felt better in her life. God, being with Colton was everything she'd ever hoped and fantasized—and more. Almost her entire life, Colton Brooks had been the man of her dreams, *and now* she knew he was also capable of providing her with the means of experiencing every desire she had.

Without a doubt, she'd never had a more erotic or more satisfying sexual experience in her life. And more than that, she'd had it with someone she knew and cared about and respected, someone she already clicked with in so many other ways. Even when they drove each other crazy, it was still fun in an exasperating way. She wanted more than just this one moment with Colton, but she had no idea how that might even work—or if Colton would want the same.

She hadn't forgotten his warning that relationships freaked him out. It made her heart hurt to know that all the crap with his parents had scarred him so badly, but she understood. His parents had come to some of her family's barbecues and parties when she was a kid, and she'd seen for herself how they'd ignore each other, make snide comments in joking form, or outright criticize each other in front of everyone. And she knew from things Tyler had said and from overhearing her parents' conversations that what she'd seen had just been the tip of the iceberg.

On a sigh, Kady rolled her head to the side and looked at the clock to find that it was pushing noon. Their ride would be here in three hours to take them to the airport, and they'd get on planes heading in two different directions.

Obviously they could talk on the phone or Skype or email, but an uncomfortable pressure in her chest was demanding she tell him that she wanted more now. Before something happened to burst the bubble they were in. But she also didn't want to come off as needy or clingy—she didn't want to do anything to chase his friendship away if that's all he decided he could give in the end.

Part of her desperately needed to talk to Christine, Regan, and Julie about what'd happened between her and Colton, but part of her wanted to keep it secret, private, just for them. Especially since she didn't know what it meant. If anything.

Colton returned to the bed, glorious in his nakedness. He was all long, lean muscles and golden skin. A dark smattering of hair covered his chest and led in a trail to his groin, where he was partially erect.

He crawled up between her legs and knelt. "You okay?" he asked, dark eyes boring into hers. "Too rough?"

She smiled, her heart squeezing at the concern in his voice. "I'm great. It was perfect Colton, thank you." He placed the warm cloth between her legs and she gasped, self-consciousness flooding through her for the first time. "You don't have to—"

"I want to take care of you," he said, wiping her clean and escalating the pressure in her chest. He threw the rag to the floor and climbed up behind her. "It *was* perfect," he said as he wrapped his arms around her and hauled her back against his stomach. "*You're* perfect." He pressed a kiss to her neck and her ear, and Kady turned enough so that he could kiss her on the mouth.

The kiss was sweet and tender, but no less sexy. She cupped the side of his face and stroked her fingers into his short hair. Against her hip, she felt him harden, though he made no move to act on it. Still, it made her smile.

"What?" he asked around the edge of the kiss. She shifted her hip against his length, and he grinned. "Can't help it when I'm around you. Truth be told, I've *never* been able to help it when I'm around you."

That made her smile even bigger. "Can I ask you a question?"

"Anything," he said, propping his head up on his hand.

"How did you figure out you liked...what we did?"

His fingers dragged over her belly, making small unconscious patterns that tempted her to squirm. "One time when I was on leave in Germany, a group of us went to this sex club with live demonstrations in addition to all the private playing that was going on. Some crazy shit. But there was a very intense BDSM scene going on. And watching it flipped a switch in my brain. You sure you want to know this?"

"Yes. You're thirty-two and I'm twenty-six, Colton. Both of us have had experiences before today. I can handle it."

"Okay." He winked and pressed a kiss to her temple. "A

woman saw me watching the scene and one thing led to another. She was a masochist, and frankly wanted more than I could give. But that switch of mine? Actually experiencing this for the first time permanently stuck it in the on position and made me realize that something had always been missing for me."

Kady totally understood that feeling. Something had definitely been missing for her, too, and now she knew what it was. "Pretty sure the same thing just happened to me."

Colton quirked a crooked smile, but then his face went serious. "I'm glad it was me."

"I'm glad it was you, too." Words sat on the tip of her tongue, but all she could hear was Colton telling her that the idea of long-term relationships freaked him out. She didn't want to be *that* woman—the one who had sex and then started planning a wedding.

Meeting his gaze, she gave him a small smile. He was so damn gorgeous it made her heart hurt, though his eyes were bloodshot and dark. A long moment of silence stretched out, and Kady dreaded it turning awkward. She stroked her fingers over his cheek. "You look tired. We have some time. Lay your head down," she said.

"Yeah, that sounds good." He scooted down, laid his head on her chest, and covered half her body with his, his thigh across hers, his arm thrown across so he could tuck his hand beneath her. He let out a sigh of pure exhausted pleasure. "You mind?" he asked, a bit of a humor in his voice.

Kady chuckled. "I suppose I can put up with it." In truth, she adored it.

"Your fault I was up all night reading," he mumbled.

Heat filled her cheeks again, and Colton was right—

it was ridiculous that his discovery of her stash of erotic romance made her react that way after everything else that'd happened. "Exactly how much did you read?" she asked.

"Pretty much everything from the scene in the alley 'til the end."

"Ohmigod," she said under her breath, thinking through all the filthy scenes that included. Her stomach flip-flopped.

He squeezed his arm around her. "Luckiest thing that ever happened," he said in almost a slur.

The words seeped from his mouth right through her skin and into her heart. If he really believed that, maybe he was feeling some of the same things she was—that she wanted more, that she didn't want this to end. Really, there was only one way to find out. "I don't want this to be it, Colton." Her pulse tripped into a sprint at the declaration.

No answer, unless the slow, deep inhale of his breathing counted. He'd fallen asleep. And as much as it sucked that she'd found the courage to say something after he'd passed out, the fact that this big, strong man had found the comfort and solace of sleep on her body was the sweetest satisfaction.

With him lying all over her like this, she couldn't not touch him. She brushed her hand over his hair, stroked his back, and ran her fingers along his arm. Above all the questions about what might or might not happen between them that ran through her head was the feeling of absolute rightness about what they'd done, and what they were doing right now.

That feeling of rightness spread over her even more completely than Colton. And Kady resolved to say something before they left today.

• • •

A musical ringtone played way in the distance, hauling Colton out of sleep. His mind rose slowly into consciousness, resisting and regretting being pulled from the best sleep he'd had in days. Maybe longer.

As soon as his mind broke the surface, he realized he'd been hearing the ring of his cell. Panic flashed through him. What time was it?

He lifted his upper body and his eyes tracked to the clock on the nightstand. Two thirty. Damnit. The ringing cut out and Colton groaned. They needed to be dressed, packed, and read to go in a half hour.

Staring down at the naked woman sprawled on the bed, Colton admired Kady's beauty. The combination of her black hair, pale skin, and dark-pink lips was alluring and so damn appealing to him he didn't want to look away. But the time didn't give him a choice.

His stomach churned and burned over exactly he wanted to say to her.

Colton kissed Kady's forehead. "Wake up, cupcake," he said, loving how the mere mention of his longtime nickname usually piqued her ire.

"Are you really still gonna call me that?" she asked, coming awake on a smile. Her eyes were soft and warm and gentle as they focused on him.

Man, how he'd love to wake up to her every day. It made his cock harden just to imagine it. "Of course I am," he said. "Nothing has to change."

Kady blanched, then Colton literally saw as she shut

down her reaction to his comment and brightened her expression again. She looked away. "Oh my God, is that the time?" She rolled out of the far side of the bed, avoiding Colton all together. "Shit, shit, shit."

"Yes, that's why I woke you," he said, analyzing what had caused that momentary reaction. And then his mind repeated his own words back to him. "Kady, I didn't mean—"

"Listen, we don't have to do a whole postmortem," she said. "And we don't have time right now anyway. Mind if I grab a quick shower first?"

"No," he said as his shoulders fell. Kady grabbed her purse and disappeared into the bathroom, the door closing behind her.

As much as he'd needed the sleep and sleeping with Kady had been amazingly restful, Colton was irritated with himself for wasting his remaining time with her. They could've spent the afternoon making love, talking, a thousand things that were way better and more productive than sleep. He stalked to his cell on the dresser and check who'd called, then pressed the button to listen to his voicemail message.

It was the private confirming that one highway was good to go and he'd be here to retrieve them at fifteen hundred. So Colton was definitely out of time.

When the shower water came on, Colton knew he didn't want to leave things between them so unclear and unspecified—no way he wanted her a thousand miles away wondering if he wanted her.

He marched across the room and into the bathroom, not even bothering to knock.

"We need to talk," Colton said to the closed shower curtain as he leaned his bare ass against the counter and crossed his arms.

The edge of the curtain whipped back and Kady poked her head through. "Uh, taking a shower here."

He smirked at her and forced himself to resist the urge to lick the droplets of water from her lips. "Yes, well, fortunately, you're very bright and able to multitask, and I've already seen all your beautiful parts."

She rolled her eyes and tugged the curtain closed again. "Okay, so, what do you want to talk about?"

One beat passed, then another, and then Colton laid himself on the line. "I want us to try being together," he said, his heart racing in his chest. "I want us to figure out how to make that work. If you want to, of course."

This time, the curtain eased open much slower. Kady met Colton's gaze, and her eyes were so bright with excitement. "Really? Yes, I definitely do," she said. "Do you mean, like, a long-distance relationship? Because I've got a ton of frequent-flier miles. Or we could drive and meet in the middle, or—"

"I appreciate that, but if we could find a way, I'd love to avoid the long-distance thing," he said, crossing the room so he could stand right in front of her. "First, because after eight years in the army, I've had my fill of long-distance everything. Second, because I'm a novice at relationships and I don't want to screw it up. And, third and most importantly, because I don't want to be away from you that much."

A sweet smile played around her lips at his words. "What's the alternative, then?"

Colton braced himself and uttered the invitation that he wasn't sure why he'd never issued before. "Come work for me. As my partner. The two of us together? We'd be unbeatable. The job would bring you back to Boulder and we could be together."

Man, was Logan—Colton's college roommate and his best friend back in Boulder ever since—gonna have a field day with this development when Colton told him what was going down. But Colton didn't even care about the hardcore razzing he had coming from all his buddies because he felt the rightness of this idea down deep.

Kady's mouth dropped open. She shut the water off, grabbed a towel, and opened the curtain all the way. Her gaze dragged over his nakedness, and it said something about how important his invitation was to him that he didn't immediately focus in on her feminine interest. She squeezed the water out of her hair with the towel. "But...but...but we'd kill each other within three days. We always pick on each other. And if I land this contract, I'll get a promotion."

"I'm offering you a promotion," he said. "A big one. To partner. That's not something you're going to get at Resnick, no matter how many contracts you land. I need a partner, Kady, and you're the best there is. And we won't kill each other. We've always clicked around the work, and you know it."

Dried off now, Kady wrapped the towel around her body and stepped out onto the bath mat so that they were almost toe-to-toe. "It's an amazing offer, Colton. Really. But what happens if I quit my current job and took this one, and then you and I..."

Colton didn't like any of the ways he thought she might've intended to conclude that question. But he couldn't say it was an unfair concern. "My gut's telling me that's not a problem, Kady, because we fucking *click*. But even if things didn't work out, this offer is in no way contingent on us having a relationship. In fact, I'd first thought about this yesterday before anything happened between us. You're too good for Resnick, and you're sure as shit too good to have to deal with Bob Chase. We'd be professionals, and your job would be safe no matter what. But if things didn't work out and you wanted to move on, I'd make sure there was a generous severance package in your contract, just like you'd get anywhere." He stood in front of her and swiped a droplet of water running down her temple with his thumb. "All these things we can work out, but first you just have to agree."

Kady's eyes went glassy. "This is...I'm overwhelmed, Colton. Honestly. I respect you so much, and the thought that you'd want me to work at the company you've built over the last two years is such a wonderful compliment. But I just...I can't....I need time to think about all this."

The one thing they didn't have—at least not today. But Colton nodded and slid his fingers around the back of her neck. He massaged her there, loving the way she went soft and pliant under his touch. "Of course." He kissed her, needing to taste, needing to claim, needing her on his skin and in his mouth and in his *life*. And needing to remind her how good they were together. "But remember where I started this conversation—I want a chance for us to be something."

She smiled. "I want that, too."

He kissed her cheek. "I better jump in real quick," he said, and then he turned on the water.

They'd talked just long enough that everything after that was a mad dash to get ready. Understandably, Kady didn't want to look like she'd just rolled out of bed when she saw Beckstein. Given the little weasel's comments at breakfast this morning, Colton didn't blame her.

When they were ready to go, Kady reached for the door.

Colton blocked it with his hand. He eased her around until her back settled against the cold metal. God, she was gorgeous, and he wanted her even though his gut did a free fall when he thought about what it would be like if he got her to agree. "Promise me you'll think about what I said."

A quick nod as she met his gaze. Instinct told him he wasn't imagining the warm affection pouring from her eyes for him. "Of course I will. It's all I can think about right now."

"Good." He gave her a quick kiss on the lips, but not anything that would disturb the lipstick she'd just applied. "Because I'm going to be a fucking crazy man until you give me your answer."

Her grin was immediate. She tapped a finger to her lips. "Hmm…torturing Colton…that sounds like incentive to drag things out," she said, eyes full of mischief.

Oh, how he'd love to make her pay for that. And he would. He just had to have faith that she'd find her way to the same conclusion he had—they were something special together. "Troublemaker. Out with you already," he said, opening and holding the door for her.

# Chapter Eight

Longest. Van ride. Ever.

As they finally pulled into the small airport, Kady couldn't decide which part of the trip had been more torturous. Spending a hundred minutes locked in a small space with Albert Beckstein, who took a half dozen calls on which he acted like a prick and talked way too freaking loud?

Or maybe getting bounced over ruts in the terrible roads made harder to navigate by the huge puddles that congregated everywhere along their trip? There were only two places where they had to slow almost all the way down to cross a deeper pool of standing water, but even the smaller puddles were hell because they hid potholes in the road.

Or possibly, sitting in a small space with Colton Brooks while not being able to touch him or tell him how much his offer and his words meant to her? Worse, she'd had to shut him down when he'd tried to whisper something about his offer to her early on in their trip. No way she was chancing Beckstein knowing something had happened between them in the past twenty-four hours.

Bad enough guys in the industry made cracks about her exchanging sexual favors to get the things she got in her career; she didn't need Beckstein being armed with any actual proof.

So it was hands off as long as he was within earshot or sight. Which made Kady ache. Her hand itched to hold Colton's. Her body yearned to feel his against her. Her lips longed for his kiss. She just wanted to curl up in the warm, strong shelter of Colton's lap and stay there forever.

And it seemed like he'd given her a way to make that happen. Kady was still reeling from his offer. Professionally, it was an amazing opportunity. She could finally be her own boss and lead up her own projects. Brooks Computer Security Services wasn't as large a firm as Resnick, but Colton's military experience had given him a very lucrative niche and the contracts flowed his way one after the other.

Personally, taking Colton up on his offer would allow her to move back home and be closer to her family. Not spending as much time with them was something she regretted about living so far away. She was a little concerned about how her roommate might react to the idea of her moving, but no doubt she'd absolutely squee when she found out that Kady and Colton had hooked up after a lifetime of her wanting him and thinking he was outside her reach.

Finally—and most importantly—she'd get to explore this thing with Colton. Her gut said the same as his—that they were too well matched and had too much history for any relationship they might have to totally crash and burn.

But if the worst did happen, it would be disastrous on so many levels. That wasn't necessarily a reason not to give it a try, but she needed to think all of the possible fallout through before she could truly decide.

Plus, a part of her was balking at the idea of moving for someone she'd only just begun to date…or see…or whatever it was they were maybe possibly doing. Then again, she'd known Colton almost her whole life, had had feelings for him for at least half of it, and now knew he had feelings for her, and had for some time. Couldn't that be enough of a foundation? Couldn't that be enough off which to take a leap of faith? Wasn't Colton worth the risk?

Damn, she had a lot of phone calls to make when she got home! Her girls were going to *flip*.

Those questions lingered in her mind as the van finally pulled into the small terminal. It was only a matter of moments before they unloaded and made their way inside. And just because Kady wasn't in any hurry to part from Colton, they sailed right through check-in and security.

The only thing going their way was that Beckstein didn't seem to want to hang around them any more than they wanted to be in his presence. He took off for his gate the moment he had his shoes back on.

"Well," Kady said, sadness slinking into her gut. "I don't know what to say. Everything that comes to mind seems inadequate or silly."

Colton smiled, but she didn't think she was imagining the sadness in the set of his eyes and mouth, too. "Yeah. Know just what you mean. Have a bite to eat with me before you go?" he asked.

Regret weighted down her shoulders. "I don't think I

have time. My flight will be boarding in about ten minutes."

"Oh, right. Of course. Then, when can we talk again?" he asked.

Kady's heart squeezed at his questions, because they were all evidence that he was as unprepared to part with her as she was with him. "Um, tonight when we get home? Or, really, any night this week—"

"Tonight. Done." He nailed her with a stare and arched a brow. "I'll call you around nine your time?"

"Yeah, that'll work," she said, smiling.

The three feet separating them was excruciating to bear, especially as an awkwardness settled into the air between them. Kady wanted to throw herself at Colton, climb up his body, and kiss him silly. But this airport wasn't that big, and she wasn't sure exactly how close Beckstein's gate might be. God, she wouldn't put it past him to be hiding behind some potted plant with his camera phone at the ready.

"Okay, then. I'll talk to you tonight, cupcake," he said with a wink. And then he leaned down and gave her the quickest of pecks on the cheek.

Kady rested a hand on his chest before he pulled fully away. "I really want to kiss you," she whispered. "But thank you for understanding why I can't."

"I'd do anything to protect you," he said, patting her hand where it laid on him.

Her heart and stomach both ached with icy dread as the moment of separation approached.

And then Colton was saying good-bye and walking away across the concourse, other travelers interrupting her line of sight of his tall, broad back until she couldn't see him anymore. Whether he'd meant to or not, he'd taken her heart with her. What else would explain the hollow, aching emptiness she felt inside her chest?

An incredible sensation of loss swamped her, but Kady forced her feet to move as she went in the opposite direction in search of her gate, which of course ended up being at the very end of the terminal. On the way to the airport, she'd been hungry, but now the restaurants she passed along the way held absolutely no interest for her. Because the only thing that would satisfy her right now was having Colton back in her arms.

*Then just say yes.*

She couldn't decide this so quickly, though, could she? There were pros and cons to be argued, arrangements and logistics to be considered, and details to be hammered out.

True. Except on some level her gut said none of that mattered. Not a single bit.

*You already know how you feel, Kady. How you've always felt.*

Also true.

*So what are you going to do?*

• • •

Being in the Army meant that Colton had had to say a lot of good-byes over the years. None had been harder than the one he'd just said to Kady Dresco.

Dropping heavily into a seat at his gate, Colton settled his laptop bag at his feet. His plane would start boarding in forty minutes, so at least he didn't have long to wait.

Colton felt a whole lot like someone had parked a mainframe computer on his chest. The farther he got from

Kady, the harder it was to breathe, and the more an aching pain radiated out from his chest.

Ridiculous reaction, maybe, or maybe it made perfect sense. After all, how was it supposed to feel when you'd just left the woman you realized you're in love with less than a few hours after making the realization? And now he didn't know when he'd see her again.

Needing to distract himself from missing and wanting Kady, Colton pulled out his smartphone and scrolled through his email in-box. He had a message from Colonel Jepsen. Anticipation squeezing his gut, Colton opened it. As his eyes skimmed over the words, he wasn't sure to whether to laugh or get down on his knees and thank God.

Jepsen's team liked some parts of his proposal and some parts of Kady's. Before they decided which to go with, Jepsen wondered if Colton would be willing to consider sharing the contract such that he and Kady would each head up different parts of the work.

If this wasn't the universe giving them a giant shove in a particular direction, Colton didn't know what was.

And now the feeling of missing her was that much stronger. How would Kady react when she received this message?

Damnit. Colton wanted to know—no, he *needed* to know—what she was thinking, especially given this new news.

But it wasn't just about the job that he wanted to talk. He hadn't told her everything he should—namely, he'd never told her exactly how he felt.

Would telling her help her decide or just make the situation that much more confusing?

Certainty flooded through him—if this was a fight, he

needed every weapon he could get to win her over—and that meant being honest with his feelings. They needed it, she deserved it, and he couldn't have meant it more. Amazing how he'd gone thirty-two years before he'd fallen in love—most of that time wondering if he ever would. Now that he had, his heart was in an urgent rush to let the girl know and get her by his side.

Looking at his watch, Colton found he probably had about five minutes to locate Kady's gate before she'd be on the plane and beyond his reach. He was on his feet and moving almost immediately. Across the aisle from his gate, he spied Beckstein seated and working on his laptop. Perfect, now Colton knew he wouldn't be anywhere near them when he talked to Kady. Walking at first, then more briskly, and then finally breaking into a run, Colton didn't care about the looks and stares he was getting.

His phone rang in his pocket. Figures someone would be calling now, but Colton couldn't take the time to deal with whoever that was. He had to get to Kady before she got on her plane and put a whole lot of airspace between them.

Colton skidded to a halt in front of the bank of monitors, looking for the gate from which the San Francisco flight departed. Gate B-15, which was all the way down the far end of the hallway. Good thing he kept in shape. He took off running again, just as his phone rang for a second time.

As he dodged parents with strollers and people wearing headphones and small families meandering at almost a leisurely pace, Colton strained to see Kady's gate number as he rushed through the crowd. Finally, the sign came into view, and Colton's heart nearly sank to the floor for the fact that there were only a few passengers remaining in line.

"Kady?" he yelled in case she was one of them. "Kady!"

She stepped out from behind a column, her phone to her ear. Her arm eased down and she slid her phone in her purse. "Colton?"

*Oh, thank God.*

"Beckstein's at the other end of the airport" was all he said as he stalked right up to her. Then he swept her into his arms and kissed her as if he was trying to make up for every other time he'd wanted to do this but couldn't. Kady's arms came up around his neck and Colton groaned in triumph as he held her tight against his chest. It felt so damn good to have her in his arms that he wasn't sure how he'd survived the past few hours of not touching her. Their lips pulled, tongues twirled, and hands grabbed tight. The passion and desire in this kiss alone gave Colton the confidence he needed to know that what he'd offered her would never turn out to be a mistake.

"I'm so—" she began just as he said, "I realized—"

They both laughed, and Colton took Kady's beautiful face in his hands. "I realized I forgot to tell you something very important that might help you make your decision." His heart was a bass drum pounding in his chest.

"Okay," Kady said, smiling broadly. He didn't think he was imagining the hope and relief shining from her eyes.

"I love you." A weight lifted from his chest at expressing what he felt. "I don't know when it started. Maybe that night three years ago when I decided I'd have to be satisfied with loving you from afar. Or maybe it was some other time altogether. All I know is that being with you this weekend awakened feelings that had been all boxed up inside me and now they're all I can think about. I love you, Kady."

Kady's eyes went glassy but there was so much happiness radiating from her face. "Oh my God, I can't believe this is happening," she said, pressing a kiss into one of his palms. She stepped into him and laid her hands on his chest. "I've loved you my whole life, Colton. You're the only man I've ever wanted. And I love you, too."

Satisfaction and relief and a thousand other feelings he couldn't sort out surged through Colton's body. She loved him. She loved him, too.

Tears leaked from the corners of Kady's eyes.

"Aw, don't cry," he said.

"Can't help it," she said through a watery smile that turned into a small laugh. "I'm so happy I can't hold it all inside."

Colton tugged her into his chest and held her tight. For a long moment, they just stood there, totally wrapped in each other and in the feelings they both shared.

"Did you get an email from Jepsen?" he asked against her hair.

She nodded. "I was trying to call you."

Colton smiled. And he'd been irritated at his phone ringing. "So, what do you think?"

"Miss, if you're getting on the plane, you have to do it now," the gate attendant called.

Kady pulled out of his embrace and looked over her shoulder. "I'll be right there." She tilted her head back to meet his gaze again. "I think the universe might be sending us a sign."

He threw his head back on a laugh. "I thought the very same thing. So then, what do you say, Kady? Say you'll come be with me. Say you'll come work with me. Say you'll let me love you. Just say yes."

"Miss, we're about to close the door on the plane," the woman called again.

Bright-green eyes stared up at him. Kady nodded. "Yes," she said in a choked voice. "I have a lot to figure out, but I don't have to think about this—about you—a minute more. So, yes."

Colton lifted Kady in his arms and spun her around, making her laugh. "Oh, I'm so damn glad."

"Me, too," she said.

Colton gave her a quick kiss, still hating to let her go but feeling a lot more settled about where things stood. The rest would fall into place—he'd make sure of it. "Okay, go. I'm still calling you tonight, and we can start putting some plans into place."

Walking backward toward the gate, Kady nodded. "Okay. God, I don't want to leave you."

Damnit, he didn't want that either. He was already scanning through the schedules of the upcoming weekends to see when he could fly out to see her. This Saturday's rock-climbing plans were definitely getting postponed, but Colton knew Logan would understand. "This isn't good-bye. One way or the other, I'll see you soon."

She smiled and turned away, giving the agent her boarding pass to scan. "I'm really sorry," Kady said.

The agent leaned closer. "Don't be, honey. If that man had just told me he loved me, we'd be heading to a hotel."

Kady burst out laughing and looked with wide eyes and a reddening face to Colton.

"Smart woman," he said with a grin and a nod.

Both the agent and Kady laughed. "Best hurry now," the

attendant said.

Kady gave a wave as she stepped through the door and onto the gangway.

"Hey, Kady?" Colton called.

She turned and smiled, her face absolutely radiant.

"Just be ready for me, sweetheart. Because this isn't the last time you're going to say yes to one of my questions." He winked.

"We'll just see about that, Brooks," she called as she blew a kiss and ran down the hall.

As the agent closed the door, Colton stood there smiling. He'd never felt happier than he did at this moment, because the last and most important piece of the puzzle of his life had finally clicked into place.

And though he already missed Kady, Colton was content. Because separating right now represented their beginning, not their end.

***Grab the rest of the Wedding Dare series!***

When four bridesmaids dare one another to find lust—or maybe even love—at the destination wedding event of the year, the groomsmen don't stand a chance. But little do the women know, the men are onto their game, and sparks will fly alongside the bouquet.

Four bridesmaids. Four groomsmen.
Five *New York Times* and USA TODAY bestselling authors. Long-carried torches, sizzling new attractions, and forbidden conquests will ensure a wedding never to be forgotten.

### BAITING THE MAID OF HONOR
a *Wedding Dare* novel by Tessa Bailey

Julie Piper and Reed Lawson are polar opposites. She's a people-pleasing former sorority girl. He's a take-no-prisoners SWAT commander who isolates himself from the world. But when they're forced together at their friends' posh destination wedding and she's dared to seduce another man, Reed takes matters into his own hands. One night should be all he needs to get the blond temptress out of his system, but he's about to find out one taste is never enough...

### FALLING FOR THE GROOMSMAN
a *Wedding Dare* novel by Diane Alberts

Photojournalist Christine Forsythe is ready to tackle her naughty to-do list, and who better to tap for the job than a hot groomsman? But when she crashes into her best friend's older brother, her plans change. Tyler Dresco took her virginity during the best night of her life, then bolted. The insatiable heat between them has only grown stronger, but Christine wants revenge. Soon, she's caught in her own trap of seduction. And before the wedding is over, Tyler's not the only one wanting more…

## SEDUCING THE BRIDESMAID
### a *Wedding Dare* novel by Katee Robert

Regan Wakefield is unafraid to go after what she wants, so she's thrilled when her friend's wedding offers her an opportunity to score Logan McCade, the practically perfect best man. Unfortunately, groomsman Brock McNeil keeps getting in her way, riling her up in the most delicious of ways. Regan may pretend the erotic electricity sparking between them is simply a distraction, but Brock will do whatever it takes to convince Regan that the best man for her is *him*.

## BEST MAN WITH BENEFITS
### a *Wedding Dare* novel by Samanthe Beck

Logan McCade's best man duties have just been expanded. Coaxing his best friend's little sister out of her shell should be easy for a high-octane extrovert like himself—or so he thinks until he's blindsided by the delectably awkward Sophie Brooks. She's sweet, sexy, and brings much-needed calm to his hectic life. Soon, he's tempting her to explore all her forbidden fantasies… and wondering exactly how far a favor to his best friend can go.

# Acknowledgments

A huge thanks to Heather Howland, Katee Robert, Tessa Bailey, Samanthe Beck, and Diane Alberts for including me in this wonderfully fun continuity project. The other authors had by far the harder job of coordinating four awesome stories, leaving me with the icing on the cake (wedding cake, of course!) in getting to write the story of how Colton and Kady got together.

A big thanks also to Lea Nolan, Jennifer L. Armentrout, Christi Barth, and Stephanie Dray for providing tons of encouragement and support along the way. A writer couldn't ask for better friends.

And of course, thanks to my amazingly patient family for always supporting my dreams so I can do this wonderful work I love so much.

Finally, thanks to the readers, who welcome characters into their hearts and minds and let them tell their stories over and over again. ~ LK

# About the Author

Laura is the *New York Times* and USA Today bestselling author of over a dozen books in contemporary and paranormal romance and romantic suspense. Growing up, Laura's large extended family believed in the supernatural, and family lore involving angels, ghosts, and evil-eye curses cemented in Laura a lifelong fascination with storytelling and all things paranormal. She lives in Maryland with her husband, two daughters, and cute-but-bad dog, and appreciates her view of the Chesapeake Bay every day.

www.LauraKayeAuthor.com

*Discover Laura Kaye's NYT bestselling* **Heroes series...**

## HER FORBIDDEN HERO

Former Army Special Forces Sgt. Marco Vieri has never thought of Alyssa Scott as more than his best friend's little sister, but her return home changes that. Now that she's back in his life, healing wounds he never thought would heal, will he succumb to the forbidden temptation she presents one touch at a time?

## ONE NIGHT WITH A HERO

After growing up with an abusive, alcoholic father, Army Special Forces Sgt. Brady Scott vowed never to have a family of his own. But when a one-night stand with new neighbor Joss Daniels leads to an unexpected pregnancy, can he let go of his past and create a new future with Joss?

### *More Entangled books by Laura Kaye*

NORTH OF NEED
WEST OF WANT
SOUTH OF SURRENDER
EAST OF ECSTASY

CPSIA information can be obtained
at www.ICGtesting.com
Printed in the USA
BVOW03s1836271217
503813BV00001B/3/P